"I'm not dumb enough to have an affair with you."

Nick had the grace to look ashamed of himself, then abruptly he grinned. "It sounded like fun to me."

"I'm sure it did," Chelsea snapped. "And it probably would be even more fun when you could fire me next week."

"Why would I want to do that? You're actually quite good at what you do."

"I suppose it should be some comfort that you've finally noticed!"

Nick frowned. "I don't quite understand why you turned me down, you know. Frankly, Burke is getting old. His name doesn't carry the same weight it used to in the field. I think you'd be wise to look around for a new patron."

The look Chelsea gave him should have shriveled him completely.

Books by Leigh Michaels

HARLEQUIN PRESENTS
702—KISS YESTERDAY GOODBYE
811—DEADLINE FOR LOVE
835—DREAMS TO KEEP

HARLEQUIN ROMANCE
2657—ON SEPTEMBER HILL

These books may be available at your local bookseller.

Don't miss any of our special offers. Write to us at the
following address for information on our newest releases.

Harlequin Reader Service
P.O. Box 52040, Phoenix, AZ 85072-2040
Canadian address: P.O. Box 2800, Postal Station A,
5170 Yonge St., Willowdale, Ont. M2N 6J3

LEIGH MICHAELS

dreams to keep

Harlequin Books

TORONTO • NEW YORK • LONDON
AMSTERDAM • PARIS • SYDNEY • HAMBURG
STOCKHOLM • ATHENS • TOKYO • MILAN

Harlequin Presents first edition November 1985
ISBN 0-373-10835-4

Original hardcover edition published in 1985
by Mills & Boon Limited

CHAPTER ONE

CHELSEA leaned over the draughtsman's table and pointed a pencil at the drawing he was working on, 'Jim, are you certain I put a closet in there?' she asked.

The draughtsman raised an eyebrow. 'I only follow directions, Chelsea,' he said mildly. 'I don't imagine closets. That's your department.' He finished the line that completed the closet wall and tossed his pencil down. 'What's the matter, anyway? You aren't a little nervous this morning, are you?'

'Of course not,' Chelsea jeered. 'Why would I be nervous?' Why indeed, she thought. Just down the hall, the three senior partners of the architectural firm were meeting. When they came out of that room, there would be one more partner, to fill the vacancy left by Martin Burns' sudden death three months ago. And that new partner, if she was lucky, would be Chelsea Ryan.

'Do you really think you'll get the job, Chelsea?' Jim picked up the pencil again.

'Why shouldn't I? I have as much experience as any of the other applicants. I'm a better architect than most of them, and I'm a woman, which is an image this practice could stand.'

'No fooling? You're really a woman?' Jim looked up in mock astonishment. His eyes swept over her, from auburn hair arranged in a neat and professional knot at the back of her neck to the apricot-coloured dress and delicate gold jewellery. 'By golly, you are a woman. Why didn't I ever notice?'

'Because you weren't looking before, I suppose,' Chelsea retorted. 'After all, you've only dated my roommate for a year now.'

Jim was suddenly serious. 'Just don't count on getting the job, Chelsea. The senior partners around here have never been known for liberal thinking, and they aren't apt to start now. There has never been a female partner of Shelby Harris and Associates, and you may not be the first.'

'Oh, come on, Jim, Carl Shelby himself complimented that last design of mine—the Wharton house. He called it an architectural gem.'

'And it is. Mostly because I drew it.' He preened himself playfully. 'But you're still designing houses, Chelsea.'

'What's the matter with that? I like to do houses.'

He spoke slowly, as if explaining to a kindergarten. 'The partners think that since you're a woman, that's the only thing you can be trusted with. And because none of them like residential work, they will keep palming it off on you just as long as you'll take it. Especially now that Martin's gone.'

Chelsea frowned thoughtfully. 'You may be right, Jim.'

'Of course I am. I am never wrong. I'm betting that they'll give the partnership to Owl Eyes here.' He tugged open a bottom desk drawer and pulled out a pile of sketches. The top one was a caricature of an earnest young man with horn-rimmed spectacles and a pointed nose, perched on the branch of a tree.

'You promised that you'd take those things home, Jim,' Chelsea accused.

'I forgot.' He flipped through the sheets. 'Or maybe they'll pick this one. What did you call him?'

'Granite Man,' Chelsea said automatically. 'Jim if you get caught with these . . .'

'I won't get caught.'

'That's easy for you to say. It's my name on the corner of them, and it will be my job if Carl Shelby ever sees the one of himself.' She picked up the top sketch, with her initials printed neatly in the corner, as was characteristic of all of her drawings. Granite Man stared stonily back at her from the side of Mount Rushmore, where she had neatly inserted him between the sculptured heads of Theodore Roosevelt and Abraham Lincoln.

'What's his real name?' Jim pursued. 'I've forgotten.'

'Nick Stanton. Didn't you meet him when he came for his interview? He's the original cold fish. There would be no bending the rules with him around, that's certain.'

'And Chelsea does like to bend the rules. That's probably why you won't get the partnership. That and your age. And the red hair.'

'It's auburn. Besides, what does the colour of my hair have to do with it?'

Jim shrugged. 'Little things often do. You know Carl Shelby has a million prejudices, and that Frank Harris goes along with anything Shelby wants.'

'Well, Burke Marshall doesn't.'

'Wow. One out of three, and you were always Burke's favourite. It's no majority, Chelsea.'

'Why did it have to be Martin who died? He was the easiest of them all to work with,' Chelsea said thoughtfully.

Jim grinned. 'Sure, because he was always too busy to worry about what you were doing, so you did things the way you wanted. Working for Martin was like having no boss at all.'

'He and Burke always backed me up.'

'Of course they did. But that's not the kind of behaviour that wins you a popularity contest, Chelsea. Harris and Shelby don't think anyone under fifty has learned enough about life to be rewarded with a partnership.'

'Well, that leaves out about half of their applicants. Including Granite Man.' Chelsea slid the sketch to the bottom of the stack.

'I'll take those home, just as soon as you finish the set,' Jim offered cheekily. 'I want to see what you can do with Eileen.'

Chelsea stared at him for a long moment. 'If I draw Eileen, will you promise to get these things out of the office?'

'Boy Scout's Honour.'

'Then give me a sheet of paper.'

Her pencil hovered over the sheet for several seconds, as Chelsea thought about Eileen, who was the newest of the secretaries. Then the needle-sharp point began to move. Chelsea didn't know where the caricatures came from; they just seemed to flow from her pencil, leaving her as surprised as any observer.

Jim laughed as he watched Eileen take shape on the paper, the buxom blonde in a tight sweater and painfully high heels, bending seductively over the copy machine while Carl Shelby himself stared down her neckline.

'There,' Chelsea said and tossed her pencil down.

'I'm surprised you didn't put Frank Harris in there too. He certainly spends enough time studying Eileen's architecture.' Jim leered.

Chelsea shrugged. 'I hadn't noticed.' She pushed the sketch across the drawing board. 'Now you have enough blackmail material on me for a lifetime. And that's the last piece you're going to get, too.'

'You didn't sign it,' he objected.

Chelsea sketched her interconnected initials on the corner of Eileen's short skirt and handed it back to Jim.

'I'm going to paper a wall with these someday,' he announced. 'After you're famous, of course.'

From the doorway Chelsea's secretary spoke disapprovingly. 'Miss Ryan, your new clients are here.'

Chelsea glanced at her delicate wristwatch. 'I forgot all about them, Marie.'

Jim scrambled the caricatures together and slid them into the bottom drawer. 'I'll have the drawings of the Emerson house for you this afternoon, Chelsea.'

'That will be fine, Jim,' She followed Marie down the hall.

Without looking up from her typewriter, the secretary said, 'I showed them into your office and brought them coffee, Miss Ryan.'

'Thank you, Marie,' Chelsea said gently. It was unfortunate for Marie, she thought, that she had inherited Chelsea as a boss when Martin Burns died. Marie didn't approve of the cut of Chelsea's clothes, or her informal office manners, or the style of her hair. In fact, there was almost nothing about Chelsea that Marie approved at all.

The couple waiting in Chelsea's office were in their mid-fifties. Mr Sullivan's face was ruddy and his suit expensive but not well fitted. Mrs Sullivan's hair was elaborately coiffed in a style totally unsuited to her face.

Chelsea felt a familiar sinking sensation in the pit of her stomach, and turned on the charm. 'Good morning,' she said warmly, 'I'm sorry to keep you waiting.'

Mr Sullivan got reluctantly to his feet to take her outstretched hand. 'Is it going to be much longer before Mr Ryan gets here?' he demanded. 'I'm a busy man.'

It wasn't the first time a client had assumed that she was another secretary; far too many of them thought that no woman—especially a young very petite redhead—could possibly be an architect. 'I am Chelsea Ryan,' she said gently.

Mrs Sullivan looked offended. 'Oh, no. There must be some mistake.'

If there is, Chelsea thought wryly, my parents would probably like to hear about it.

'Our friends' house was designed by C. J. Ryan,' Mrs Sullivan said. 'I saw the name on the blueprints.'

'And who were the friends, Mrs Sullivan?' When she heard the name, Chelsea smiled in brief satisfaction. That was one of her best houses. If the Sullivans wanted something like that . . .

But there was a standard answer for clients who wanted a male architect, and arguing with them about her qualifications, no matter how superior, wasn't the way to convince them. Chelsea reached for the notepad and pen which Marie had left ready on the corner of her desk and sat down in a comfortable chair. 'I'm sure if you'd prefer having a man design your house that any of our other staff architects would be happy to help you,' she said, her low voice musical. 'Unfortunately, they are all busy at the moment, and I'm afraid your trip would be wasted. So—since you're already here—why don't you tell me about the house you have in mind, and then I can pass that along to whichever of our staff you choose.'

And he, she thought rebelliously, will take one look at it and say, 'Oh, go ahead, Chelsea, design it yourself. I'll put my name on it if it will make the client happy, but I get so bored with houses.' Yes, she thought, Jim was right. She was a member of this staff because no one else liked to do the residential work. Fortunately for her, she did like it.

She thought for a moment she had lost them. Mrs Sullivan's lips were tightly compressed, and Chelsea wouldn't have been surprised if she had insisted on seeing another architect that very minute. Then Mr Sullivan stirred restlessly and said to his wife, 'Doris, I took the day off for this, you know, I hate to waste the time.'

Chelsea didn't wait for the argument to start. 'Are there just the two of you?' she inquired gently.

Mrs Sullivan nodded reluctantly. 'Our children have all moved away.'

'Tell me about yourselves,' Chelsea urged. 'Your jobs and your hobbies, the kind of entertaining you do—all that sort of thing.'

She listened for what seemed an hour, asking a question here and there, jotting down facts and ideas in the pidgin shorthand that made sense only to her. 'That brings us to the kitchen, Mrs Sullivan,' she said finally. 'Do you prefer a large one with plenty of room for projects, or a small, efficient one that is easier to keep clean?'

Mrs Sullivan looked at her with hard-won respect in her eyes. 'You really do know about houses, don't you?'

Chelsea nodded. 'I've designed hundreds. They're my favourite things to do.'

Marie tapped on the door and came in to hand Chelsea a note. She unfolded it and her heart started to pound. Burke Marshall, her favourite of the senior partners, had invited her to lunch at his club. Could she be ready in twenty minutes?

She nodded her answer to Marie, who went out as noiselessy as she had come in. But Chelsea's heart was still racing. Having lunch with any or all of the senior partners was nothing unusual, but today . . . It must mean that the decision had been made.

She pulled her mind back to the Sullivans, glancing over her notes to see if all of her questions had been answered, and clipped the sheets to the sketch they'd brought of their land. 'I'll go look at your lot this week,' she promised. 'As soon as I've seen it, I can put together some tentative drawings. I'll call you when they're ready.'

'Will you need me any more?' Mr Sullivan asked grumpily. 'I can't take too much time off. This house is for Doris, anyway. I couldn't care less where I live.'

'We have a whole chain of retail stores,' Mrs Sullivan said proudly. 'They keep Charles very busy.'

Discount outlets, no doubt, Chelsea told herself. Then, sternly, she reminded herself that the Sullivans deserved the best she could do for them. If it turned out that they wanted a one-room tar-paper shack, it

would at least be the best tar-paper shack Chelsea
Ryan could design.

'As a matter of fact, we will need you, Mr Sullivan,'
she said quietly. 'But perhaps we can meet in the
evening so that it doesn't inconvenience you.'

He finally unbent. 'That would be very thoughtful,
Miss Ryan. Doris has always wanted to live out where
there are some honest-to-goodness trees,' he added a
little stiffly. 'We've had that piece of land for years,
but it's only now that we can build on it. And she's
going to have the house she wants. She's waited long
enough for it, that's sure.'

'And you'll have the very best house we can build,
Mr Sullivan,' she assured him.

There was no more talk of a male architect. Chelsea
walked down the hall with them, listening to the last
few afterthoughts from Mrs Sullivan.

'I'm sure you'll think of more ideas,' Chelsea said
gravely. 'Why don't you jot them down and drop them
in the mail? I like having clients who are absorbed in
designing their own homes. They're much happier
with the results, you see.'

Mrs Sullivan glanced at the engraved business card
that Chelsea handed her, and agreed, Chelsea turned
from the door with a sigh of relief.

Burke Marshall was standing behind her, 'That was
neatly done, Chelsea,' he applauded, 'With one quick
suggestion you made her feel vitally important, and
you forestalled the hundred 'phone calls she would
otherwise have made to tell you "just one more
thing".'

'It's absolutely true, too. I do prefer clients who
really get absorbed in the planning.' She tipped her
head to one side to study Burke, tall, distinguished,
and white-haired, still slim despite his sixty years.
'Are you ready to go, Burke? I'm starving.'

'Don't you need a hat or something?'

'I'll be just a minute.' In her office again, Chelsea

adjusted her sunglasses, tipped the brim of her wide straw hat at the proper angle, and touched up her lipstick. 'This is your big day, Chelsea Ryan,' she told herself softly. 'The day you've been aiming for since college. A partnership well before you're thirty years old—who would ever have expected that?' She smiled at the excited woman in the mirror and practised a look of interested calm. She would look like that when Burke gave her the news, and he'd be amazed that she was so collected. It was fun to tease Burke; he'd been like an uncle since they'd met at her college, where he had been a guest lecturer. It had been her own qualifications that had won her the job with Shelby Harris, but Burke had been the one who gave her the chance to prove herself. And now it was Burke who had lobbied for her to get the partnership ... She should be taking him out to lunch, she thought, instead of the other way around.

Burke's club was a pillar of downtown St Louis society, and from the top-floor restaurant the view was breathtaking. Chelsea looked out over the city to the river and the sweep of gleaming stainless steel that formed the Gateway Arch, towering over the skyline. What a daring proposal it had been, back in the forties when it was designed, she thought, and wondered if she would have had the nerve to submit such an audacious design for a riverfront memorial.

'Shrimp cocktail and a chef's salad,' she told the waiter, and Burke frowned.

'Nothing more than that? You can't work all afternoon on lettuce,' he complained. 'You forget that the chef serves it in a mixing bowl,' Chelsea reminded. 'How's Helen?'

Burke shook his head. 'It's been several weeks since you saw her, hasn't it?'

'Yes. I've been awfully busy since Martin died, but that's no excuse for neglecting Helen.' She felt a twinge of guilt; Burke's wife was one of her favourite people, and since she had contracted a crippling disease, Helen seldom left the house, Chelsea tried to stop by at least once a week, but the press of work that Martin Burns had left undone was still forcing her to spend long days in the office.

'Her doctor says her spine is getting worse, and that she'll be confined to a wheelchair in another six months or so.'

'Oh, no, Burke.'

Burke nodded sadly. 'We've known it was coming, of course. She's been in more pain lately. At any rate, Chelsea, it's time to start designing our new house—one that Helen can run from the wheelchair.'

Chelsea was thinking about Hillhaven, the big old Victorian mansion that Burke and Helen had re-modelled so patiently, with love in every door frame and light switch. 'There are so many obstacles for people with physical handicaps.'

'Especially in that house. There are thresholds in every doorway, Chelsea. Helen won't even be able to get from room to room without help.'

'Being dependent on someone else would kill her, Burke.' Chelsea's mind was already busy designing a new house. Spacious enough for a wheelchair, yet compact enough to avoid fatiguing Helen . . .

'Will you do it? She's not wild about the idea just yet—I don't think she's entirely accepted the fact that the doctor knows what he's talking about. But if you had some sketches tucked away to show her just as soon as she is ready to discuss it . . .'

'Sure, Burke. I'll run something up.'

'It's going to be so hard on her,' Burke went on. 'Since she first became ill, she has managed by having the housekeeper come in a couple of days a week. It's important to her to continue being self-sufficient.'

Chelsea nodded and thoughtfully dipped a jumbo shrimp into the spicy sauce. 'If she can't run her own home anymore, she isn't going to want to fight that disease.'

'That's what scares me,' Burke said. Suddenly he looked old.

'And in that kitchen, she can't even cook from a wheelchair.' Chelsea's mind was churning. There are some new books out on designing for the handicapped, she was thinking. 'I'll see what I can come up with.'

'Nothing too elaborate at first,' Burke warned. 'I don't want her to think we've been scheming behind her back.'

'Even if we have,' Chelsea said demurely.

Burke smiled at that. 'I hope that Helen will bring it up to you herself. She loves that house, and I don't want to push her into giving it up.'

Chelsea finished her shrimp and pushed the glass aside. 'I don't suppose we could just re-model?'

Burke considered and shook his head. 'I don't see how. And let's face it, Chelsea, we bought that house thirty years ago when we thought there would be kids in every bedroom. We certainly don't need a fifteen-room Victorian mansion now.'

Chelsea shrugged. 'Needing and wanting are two different things. If I had a dollar for every client who wants a house she doesn't need . . .'

Burke laughed. 'I see your point.'

'And when I try to design the house she needs, she gets upset and finds an architect who will sell her what she wants.'

'Helen is just going to have to be practical.'

'Well, surely there's a house that she can't help but fall in love with.'

'Good girl. And stop by to see her, too. She gets lonely.' He studied her thoughtfully over the rim of his glass. 'It's just work that's been keeping you away? I thought perhaps it was a new boyfriend.'

'Nothing so original, I'm afraid.' Chelsea swirled

the ice cubes in her glass and said, with her heart in her throat, 'Burke ... how did the meeting go this morning?'

He set his cup down with a clatter. 'I'm sorry, Chelsea. I was so concerned about the new house that I forgot.' His eyes were dark. 'They made the decision, and . . .'

If it was me, Chelsea thought with sudden frozen logic, he would have said WE decided.

'I'm sorry, Chelsea. Carl and Frank think we need someone with more experience, with a broader record in public buildings, and . . .'.

'And not a woman,' Chelsea said bitterly. 'Burke, I've got the experience. And they certainly know my work. I've done plenty of it since Martin died, finishing up all his projects.'

'I know, Chelsea. You've been valuable; no one else could have stepped into Martin's shoes. We all know what a mess you inherited when he died.'

'Then how could they pass over one of their own staff to bring in an outsider?'

'Because he's one of the best-known new lights in architecture, that's why,' Burke said.

'If he's so damned good, why is he willing to move? Why does he even want a partnership? He could start his own firm.'

'Any architect would be please to join Shelby Harris. It has a national reputation, Chelsea.'

'If the partners aren't careful, Shelby Harris will be nationally known as a bigoted, discriminatory . . .'

Burke looked shocked. 'Are you saying that you might sue the firm?'

'Why shouldn't I?' Then Chelsea relented. 'No, I won't sue. I know what would happen. I'd lose, and the whole cause would be set back ten years.'

'You would lose,' Burke agreed. 'Your credentials are good, but Nick Stanton's are so outstanding that nobody could argue with the decision.'

'Stanton? They hired Granite Man?' Chelsea's tone was unbelieving.

'The entire stack of applications couldn't have beaten him if they were put together.' Then Burke said, unbelievingly, 'What did you call him?'

'Nothing important, Burke.' She bit her lip. 'You know that it's going to very hard for me to work with him. After Martin, it will be hard to have any new boss. But answering to Nick Stanton . . .'

'That's why I brought you to lunch—to talk to you before the official announcement is made. I was afraid you'd blow up in public if it took you by surprise.'

'I probably would have,' Chelsea admitted. 'When is it going to be announced, Burke?'

'Immediately, Carl called Nick this morning, and he'll start to work Monday.'

'That's prompt. Hasn't he got anything better to do than wait around for a 'phone call?'

Burke didn't answer. A fleeting look of pain crossed his face, and he said, 'You aren't going to like this, either. Helen and I are having a cocktail party this weekend to introduce him to the whole staff.'

'Traitor,' Chelsea muttered.

'I have to work with him, too, Chelsea. And even though I was promoting you for the position, I have nothing against Nick. He will add fantastic strength to the firm. So I volunteered.'

'Can Helen handle it?'

Burke shrugged. 'It will be catered. There's nothing to handle, really.'

'In that case, I won't offer to help. Let's see, what plans can I make for next weekend? I haven't been up to Norah Springs to visit my parents in a while.'

'Don't you dare,' Burke threatened. 'You have to show up at that party, Chelsea.'

'What will you do if I don't? Spank me?' Her big green eyes widened in mock fright.

'I'd be tempted, it's imperative that you swallow

this resentment, Chelsea. If you just look at it as a learning experience . . .'

'Oh, I've learned from it already. I've learned that if I want to be a partner, I'd better start checking out some different firms. Shelby Harris won't be it, that's sure.'

'Are you certain that you want to move? You have more prestige on the staff at Shelby Harris than you would as a partner anywhere else in St Louis. It's small, but there isn't a better-known firm in the whole state.'

'That's true,' Chelsea admitted grudgingly. The mere mention of Shelby Harris at a gathering of architects was enough to bring respectful silence.

'And if you insist on moving, remember that you won't get much of a reference from Nick if you can't work with the team. So dump the resentment and bite your tongue and be nice to the man, Chelsea. You might discover that he isn't so bad after all.'

'I'm not holding my breath,' Chelsea announced. 'He's got an annoying little trick of looking at a set of plans and dismissing them as if they were no better than an infant's scribble.'

'He's a good architect, Chelsea.'

'I'm not questioning his skill. But he pulled that trick on me while he was here interviewing. I had the drawings for the Wharton house on my desk and you'd have thought he'd never seen anything so dreadful.'

'Did he say anything?'

'He didn't have to. He just turned up his nose as if the drawings smelled bad.'

Burke tried to hide a smile. 'And what did you do?'

'As soon as he walked out, I put them in the wastebasket,' Chelsea admitted reluctantly.

'The set I saw was beautiful.'

'That was the second try,' Chelsea muttered. 'Carl Shelby liked them too.'

He sobered again. 'Chelsea, if you can just pretend that he's a human being ... Think what you can learn from the man. And he can't be all that hard to work for.'

'I'm not betting—but what choice do I have? I'll try, Burke. I will really try.'

Her chef's salad suddenly didn't taste very good. Chelsea made a pretence of eating, but she was relieved when Burke finally pushed his coffee cup aside and said, 'Shall we walk back to the office?'

She had kept the afternoon free of appointments so she could visit the sites of the several houses that were being built to her design around the city. Instead, she shut her office door, flung her hat and handbag into a chair, and strode over to stand by the window, her clenched hand pressed against her mouth, fighting back the tears that threatened to flow.

She had wanted that job so badly, had planned and schemed and played office politics. And they gave it to someone else. It hurt with a deep stab that nearly took her breath away. But what also hurt was the discovery that she had allowed herself to count on getting the partnership, on being one of the four people who made the policy for the firm. All the time she had been telling herself that it was a wonderful opportunity, that if she was lucky she might be selected, she had really been thinking that it was a sure thing. Now she had to readjust her whole attitude.

And instead of moving into that walnut-panelled office down the hall, she would have to walk by it and know that Nick Stanton was there instead.

He was a fantastic architect. Burke was right about that. Chelsea had seen his designs, had read the articles he submitted to the professional journals. It wasn't his talent she despised, but the man himself. He was cold and silent and supercilious and arrogant. Granite Man, she thought. There couldn't have been a better name for him.

There was a perfunctory knock and then the door opened. Chelsea wheeled around to see Jim, a set of drawings rolled up in his hand, come in.

He stopped, surprised, when he saw her. 'I thought you were going out to the sites today,' he said.

'I changed my mind. Is that my new house?'

Jim unrolled the finished work on the drawing board. 'And your rough sketches,' he said, handing her the originals. 'The elevations are all there, too.'

'Good.' She stared at the sketch of the front elevation, the house low and rambling, its wide roof overhanging the inviting front door, the big oak tree framing the view. They'd have to be careful of that tree during construction; it was one of the best features of the lot the clients had chosen, and she was not going to allow its removal. She made a mental note to talk to the contractor. 'It's a pretty house, isn't it, Jim?'

'How professional you are,' he mocked. 'With all of the terms that apply, you choose "pretty".'

'It's true,' Chelsea defended herself. 'And that's the way the clients will think of it.'

'You amaze me, Chelsea. But if it works . . .' Jim shrugged. 'Tell Judy I'll pick her up at seven.'

'Why don't you tell her yourself? You have a telephone.' Then Chelsea regretted the sharpness of her tone.

Jim just raised an eyebrow. 'The grapevine must be right. Rumour has it that you didn't get the job.'

Chelsea turned back to the window, staring out towards the wide Mississippi. She almost wanted to go jump into the water, to let the river carry her down to New Orleans. 'It's right,' she said. Dejection dripped from her voice.

'It isn't the end of the world, you know.'

'It certainly feels like it, Jim.' Her voice suddenly rose vehemently. 'I hope Nick Stanton makes such a mess of things that he's tarred and feathered before the year's out.'

Jim watched her thoughtfully for a few minutes. Then he said, 'Actually you should be praying he makes it big.'

Chelsea wheeled around. 'Why on earth?'

'Because the partners have already taken one enormous step forward by choosing him at all. He's still in his thirties, you know. And if he does well, they might be encouraged to go one step farther and give a woman a chance.'

She considered it and shook her head. 'It's going to be years before there's another vacancy in the partnership.'

'Maybe not. Nobody anticipated this one. Just watch your step, Chelsea. Something tells me that Nick Stanton isn't the kind of enemy you want to have. I'll bet he plays rough. A whole lot rougher than you can.'

CHAPTER TWO

'AREN'T you going to get dressed soon?' Judy Martin stood in the doorway between hall and living room, her hair in electric rollers, wearing a silky slip and almost nothing else.

Chelsea didn't even look up from the drawing board that was tucked into a corner of the living room. She checked a figure in the book and erased a line on her paper, wishing that she had brought home an electric eraser from the office. This new house for the Marshalls was giving her fits—she had drawn every line at least three times.

'It's only a cocktail party, Judy,' she said finally. 'You aren't dressing for dinner at the White House, you know.'

'Sometimes you infuriate me, Chelsea.' Judy put her hands on her hips. 'It's very important that I make a good impression on all those people. I'd hate to make a fool of myself by falling into the punchbowl or something.'

'There won't be a punchbowl.' Chelsea didn't sound interested. She sketched a corner of Helen Marshall's prospective new kitchen on a scrap of paper and finally looked up. 'You will not get drunk. You will not drop a glob of taco dip on to Carl Shelby's fifty-dollar tie. You will not look gauche. This is no different from the company Christmas party, for heaven's sake. You enjoyed that.'

'But it is different.' Judy sounded terrified. 'The senior partners weren't at the Christmas party. I don't know if I can handle meeting all of them at once. I mean, Shelby and Harris and Marshall!'

'You've talked to Burke dozens of times on the

'phone. Besides, all you have to do is sip a drink and bat those big blue eyes and gush, "How very interesting!" once in a while, Carl will be charmed.'

Judy didn't sound convinced. 'Will you at least come along with us?'

'I'll be there, Judy. I don't dare skip it, but I don't plan to go any earlier than I have to.'

'I don't want to walk in by myself.'

'You're going with Jim,' Chelsea pointed out. 'You won't be alone a minute.'

'But men don't understand!' Judy wailed. 'He'll just go off and get a drink and stand in a corner and talk buildings and . . .'

'And you're going to rip yourself into a small pile of shreds if you don't stop.' Chelsea put her pencil down. 'All right, if it will make you feel better. But I'm staying for dinner with Burke and Helen, so I'll take my own car. I will follow you out there and walk in with you. Is that good enough?'

Judy nodded. 'I'm sorry to be such a baby,' she said. 'It's just that elegant parties really throw me.'

'Only because you aren't used to them.' Judy looked about three years old, Chelsea thought. She was a perfectly competent young woman ninety per cent of the time, but she felt inferior to the people at Shelby Harris because they had more education. Sometimes Chelsea wanted to scream at Judy that she was worth three of them.

'Besides,' Chelsea added, 'nobody ever called Helen Marshall's parties elegant. They are, of course, but everybody has such a good time that they forget to notice.'

'It's easy for you. You know everybody.'

'Well, if you want something to make you feel better, think about Nick Stanton. He's meeting everyone for the first time.'

'Poor man.' Judy was plucking rollers from her hair. 'Jim will be here in half an hour.'

'Listen, there will be no one at that party that I want to impress badly enough to spend half an hour making myself beautiful.'

'Not even your new boss?'

'Especially not him.'

'That's what's really aggravating,' Judy scolded, back to her normal tone of voice. 'You take five minutes in the shower and another five getting dressed and everyone will tell you how lovely you are. I've spent all afternoon trying to look good and nobody will even notice.'

'Jim will.' Or I'll kill him right on the spot, Chelsea decided.

'That doesn't count. Jim has to notice; it's his obligation.' She went back into her bedroom, but her voice floated out to Chelsea. 'Are you sure my blue dress will be all right?'

'It's wonderful.' Chelsea stacked her books on the stool beside the drawing board and started for her own bedroom. Once Judy was in this frame of mind, there would be no work done. Besides, despite what she had told Judy, Chelsea had already decided that she was going to look her best for this party. She was not going to wear her heart on her sleeve; the whole staff might already know that she was disappointed because she hadn't been offered the partnership, but she would not give them the satisfaction of confirming it.

So she put on the new kelly green dress that her mother had sent her last week. It wasn't the sort of thing that Chelsea would have bought for herself, but the sequin trim brought out the sparkle in her big green eyes, and the artistically uneven hem showed off perfect legs. It was a slinky dress, and it looked marvellous on her. She tucked the auburn curls up into a twist, leaving wisps and tendrils soft around her heart-shaped face, and took special pains with her make-up. Transluscent skin that leaned towards freckles was such a pain, Chelsea thought. She had to be so careful not to get sunburn that it took much of the fun out of summer.

Cars were already clogging the driveway and lining the quiet street in front of Hillhaven when Chelsea parked her Mercedes convertible behind Jim's battered compact car. The house was tucked into one of the old residential neighbourhoods of west St Louis, where wrought-iron gates closed off the streets to keep the casual sightseer out. There had probably been more traffic in this cul-de-sac today than in the last month.

Jim looked impatient as he helped Judy out of the car. She must have been fussing about her fears throughout the drive, Chelsea knew.

Much more of that nonsense, Judy, my girl, she thought, and you may be surprised to find Jim escorting someone who does feel at ease at the office parties. And you'll be sitting at home.

She climbed the brick steps slowly, listening to the leaves that rustled on the huge old oaks beside the double front doors. The trees were still the warm yellow-green of spring. It was May, and nature again held out the promise of warmth and growth and renewal.

Jim rang the bell. Then he looked down at Chelsea and said, 'Are you nervous, too?'

'I am never nervous,' she lied bravely.

Jim hooted, but before he could answer, Burke opened the door. 'Hello, Chelsea,' he said cheerfully. 'Jim. And . . . Judy, isn't it?'

Judy looked as if she was going to shrivel up under Burke's friendly gaze.

'They're all in the drawing room,' Burke gestured towards the long French doors. A burst of laughter came from the room, and Chelsea lifted an eyebrow with an inquiring look.

'Your Mr Stanton must be the life of the party,' she said sweetly, hanging back to talk to him as Jim and Judy crossed the hall.

Burke shook a finger at her. 'Now, Chelsea,' he warned.

'Oh, I'm trying to pretend that he's human,' she added. 'Just as you requested. But it requires such a dreadful amount of concentration, you see.' She drifted into the drawing room without waiting for Burke's answer.

The room must have been forty feet long, but the proportions were so perfect that it looked comfortable and intimate. Chelsea never walked into that drawing room without hesitating an instant by the door to recognise the perfection of Helen's decorating scheme, too—the heavy Aubusson carpet laid atop a hardwood floor that was polished to a mirror gleam, the furniture scattered in casual conversational groupings, the green plants. Today, with the easy warmth of summer flowing throught the open windows, the fireplace was hidden by an elaborate needlepoint screen that mimicked the design in the carpet.

I do love Hillhaven, Chelsea thought idly. I wonder, if Burke and Helen are going to sell it, if they would make me a deal.

'Chelsea!' A low, musical voice pulled her across the room to the high-backed chair where Helen sat.

Burke was right, Chelsea thought with her first clear view of Helen Marshall. Lines of pain were written deeper than ever before into that lovely patrician face, and though she was smiling, there were faint shadows etched below her eyes. Chelsea drew a quick breath of horror. Helen's physical condition was deteriorating quickly.

Helen raised a thin hand to take Chelsea's. 'My dear, you look so lovely today,' she said. 'I want you to meet Nicholas Stanton, dear, Nick, this is Chelsea Ryan. She's a staff architect at Shelby Harris, and a particular favourite of my husband's.'

Nick Stanton hadn't warmed up a bit, Chelsea thought as she looked up at him. His deep blue eyes were just as cold, his face under the even tan just as hard, as when he had come to the office for his interview.

'We've met,' she said coolly, and offered her hand.

He shifted his glass from right hand to left after a split-second hesitation, and clasped Chelsea's fingers briefly.

If she had been trying to make a good impression on him, she would have been insulted by the mockery of a handshake. It was a good thing that she didn't really care what Nick Stanton's opinion was of her, Chelsea thought.

'Yes,' he was saying. 'I understand that Burke and Miss Ryan are . . . very close.'

Chelsea saw red. So he thought that Burke had tried to get her that partnership just because she was his protegé, did he? Well, she was going to remove that idea from his mind if she had to batter his head against the fireplace wall to do it.

'Burke is a wonderful man,' she said. 'He has given me more than I could have ever expected.'

'I've heard that,' Nick said silkily.

'I mean attention,' Chelsea stormed. 'And knowledge. Not jobs, Mr Stanton, whatever you think.'

'Chelsea is a wonderful architect, Nick,' Helen put in. 'She planned all the re-modelling we've done to Hillhaven.'

Nick raised his glass, sipped, looked at Chelsea over the rim. 'I have no doubts whatsoever about her professional standards,' he said.

Chelsea stared at him for a full minute. 'If you'll excuse me, Helen,' she said. 'I'm sure there are people

standing in line to meet Mr Stanton. I'd hate to keep
him from his adoring public.'

Her mind was whirling as she turned away.
Obviously it was going to be open warfare between
them; it was the one thing she hadn't expected. She
hadn't dreamed that Granite Man would give a damn
what she thought about him; once he had the
partnership, why should he care? And after all, it
wasn't as if Burke's partiality to her had even a breath
of favouritism about it. She was darned good at her
job, and everyone in the office knew it.

Well, if Mr Great Architect Nicholas Stanton
wanted to make a fight of it, she swore, he'd discover
that Chelsea Ryan could scrap just as hard as he could.

Burke handed her a glass of champagne. Chelsea
sipped it, and since she didn't want to answer the
question she saw in his eyes, she said, 'Helen looks
tired today.'

'She is,' he admitted. 'She's always tired now. She's
such a good sport, but it wears her out just to move
around.'

Chelsea's eyes rested thoughtfully on Helen across
the room. She hadn't moved; she sat gracefully in that
high-backed chair receiving her guests and apologising
now and then for not rising to greet them. Most of
them probably hadn't noticed the fatigue that Chelsea
saw in every line of the woman's body. They didn't
even realise that she wasn't the old Helen, the one who
could dance the night away and who never, never sat
still. Chelsea's eyes filled with tears as she watched the
gallant performance.

Then she looked away from Helen and her eyes
locked with Nick Stanton's. Was it mockery that
flashed in those deep blue eyes, she wondered, as he
watched her and Burke standing there? But there
was no time to analyse it; with a tiny shrug that
looked like disgust he turned away and spoke to Carl
Shelby.

'Your Mr Stanton doesn't like me any more than I like him,' she said.

'You don't even know each other yet.' Burke sounded irritable.

'And I have no desire to study the subject, either.'

He ignored the interruption. 'You'll have a chance to get acquainted a little later.' He set his empty glass on to the tray of a passing waiter, reached for a full one, and started to move away.

'Burke!' Chelsea's voice rose. 'What does that mean?'

But Burke just saluted Chelsea with the champagne glass and went to answer the doorbell.

There was an uncomfortable twisting sensation in the pit of Chelsea's stomach. Whatever Burke had meant, she was certain that she wasn't going to like it, Chelsea thought.

She stayed off to the side of the room, her glass of champagne going flat long before she had finished it. She had discovered years ago that the most fun to be had at a cocktail party was to stay in a corner and watch the rest of the crowd. More could be learned about a person by his conduct with a drink in his hand than in any other way, Chelsea was convinced.

Eileen, for instance. The buxom blonde had arrived alone this evening, but she was surrounded by most of the young, unattached men, and a few of the married ones as well. It was no wonder that the men were hovering, Chelsea thought. Eileen's ivory silk blouse was so tight that if she took a deep breath it would probably rip, and the neckline was enticingly low.

'I'm going to take Jim home and kill him,' Judy muttered into Chelsea's ear, and sat down on the loveseat beside her. She looked sulky, and it took Chelsea just a moment to discover why. She saw that Jim, too, was on the outskirts of the crowd that surrounded Eileen.

'Don't bother. Haven't you noticed that she isn't

paying any attention to the boys? Her mind is on bigger game.' As she watched, Eileen cast a longing look towards Nick Stanton.

'The new partner? Handsome dude, isn't he?'

Chelsea shrugged. 'If you like statues.' She finished her champagne and set the glass down on the marble-topped table beside the loveseat. A waiter replaced it with a full glass so smoothly that Chelsea didn't have a chance to tell him she didn't want any more.

'I think he is gorgeous,' Judy announced. 'I always did go for guys with black hair and blue eyes. Do you know if he's attached?'

'Who cares? Are you worried that Eileen might be wasting her time? I'm sure she'd appreciate your concern.'

Judy ignored her. 'He also has two brothers. A shame they aren't in St Louis, too. If they look like him, the three of them could take the town by storm.'

'Judy, I could have nightmares thinking about Nick Stanton in triplicate. Don't do this to me.'

Judy was still staring at Nick Stanton. 'If Jim ever finishes ogling Eileen, he's taking me out to dinner. But I'll probably starve before he notices.'

'That leaves you a choice,' Chelsea said coolly. 'You can sit here and be resentful about it, or you can go tell him that you're ready to leave.'

Judy looked horrified. 'I wouldn't dare. I wonder if I could get another glass of champagne.'

Chelsea shrugged. 'Have mine.' She handed her untouched glass to Judy.

'If you're sure you don't want it.' Judy didn't wait for an answer. She sipped the wine and looked around with a sigh. 'This is a gigantic house. I bet it's beautiful at Christmas.'

Chelsea half-closed her eyes and remembered the holidays she had spent with Burke and Helen. When Helen felt up to it, Christmas at Hillhaven was a dream world. Every year there was a different decorating theme, but always the big tree stood in the bay window in the drawing room, agleam with the precious ornaments that Helen had brought back from all over the world. The last few years, though, had been quieter.

'Do all their kids come home at Christmas?'

'They don't have any.'

Judy sipped her champagne, her face registering astonishment. 'This enormous house and no family?'

'They didn't exactly plan it that way.' Chelsea said. She felt a little defensive about Burke and Helen, as if they needed protection, which was silly. 'Helen wanted about eight kids, and Burke wanted whatever Helen did. It just didn't work out.'

'Too bad. It must take a fortune to keep this place running. Do architects make that kind of money?'

'Some of them do. Burke doesn't have to; Helen's father was a millionaire.'

'Nice for him. I wonder where the waiter went.' Judy set her empty glass down with a sigh.

'Where all good waiters go when cocktail parties are over. Back into a closet somewhere, I expect.' And not a bit too soon for her friend, Chelsea thought. With relief, she watched Jim and Judy leave a few minutes later. If Judy had indulged in one more glass of champagne, she'd probably have told Eileen exactly what she thought.

The crowd thinned out rapidly then. Chelsea was standing in the hall at the bottom of the elaborate stairway when the last of them left. Her hand unconsciously caressed the satin smoothness of the walnut woodwork as she watched Burke at the door, saying goodbye to his guests. Then she felt the weight of a stare and turned to see Nick Stanton leaning against the drawing room door, his arms folded across his chest and those big dark blue eyes focused coldly on her.

If those eyes belonged to a woman, Chelsea thought

resentfully, she'd be burned as a witch. They were
framed with a wealth of black eyelashes, for starters,
and they had an odd slant that combined with the dark
slash of eyebrows to make him look positively evil.
Right now his gaze was ice cold, and Chelsea had all
she could do to keep from shivering as he continued to
regard her unblinkingly.

'You seem to like this house, Miss Ryan,' he said
coolly. 'Or do you make a habit of checking out the
finish on everyone's woodwork?'

Chelsea looked at her hand, resting on the carved
newel post, as if surprised to find it there. 'I adore old
houses,' she said. 'And if I have a personal stake in
this one, it would be no surprise.'

'So I understand.' His voice was perfectly smooth,
but there was a slur underneath it that made Chelsea
indignant.

'I drew the remodelling plans as a special project for
Burke while I was still in college,' she said, and
wondered why she was bothering to explain.

Nick raised an eyebrow. Who cares? it seemed to
say.

'And an excellent job she did,' Burke had closed the
door. Now he crossed the hall and drew Chelsea's
hand comfortably into the crook of his arm. 'It was a
warren of little dark rooms before—typically Victorian,
you know, Nick. I would have been delighted to go
out to the suburbs and build, but Chelsea and Helen
got their heads together and outnumbered me.' He
chuckled fondly and patted Chelsea's hand.

The little black-gowned maid from the caterer's
service came down the hall. 'Dinner is served,
Madame,' she told Chelsea.

Nick's eyebrows drew together in a sharp frown.
'I'll see if Helen is ready,' he said in a voice that was
deceptively soft. His eyes snapped.

'I'll go, Nick,' Burke said. 'It takes a bit of practise
to be able to help her. You two go on into the dining

room—we don't stand on ceremony at Hillhaven anymore.'

Chelsea's fingers tapped gently on the carved newel post as she looked up at Nick. 'You're staying for dinner?'

'I was invited.' He offered his arm. 'May I escort you, Miss Ryan?' he said, and the tone was an insult.

'The dining room is three steps away. I think I can manage to stagger that far without the support of your strong arm,' Chelsea snapped. I'm going to kill Burke for this, she thought. He could at least have warned me.

And you could at least have suspected it, dummy, she thought. The guest of honour at a cocktail party would obviously be invited to dinner. Dad always told me my hard head would get me into trouble even if my red hair didn't, she reflected.

'Interesting that the maid thought you were the hostess,' Nick mused. 'Are you planning to be the lady of the house someday?'

'For God's sake, the girl made a mistake,' Chelsea said tartly. 'She was hired for the party; she can't possibly know any of us. And if you're implying that I'm here all the time, I'm not. I haven't seen Helen in weeks.'

He nodded thoughtfully, but somehow Chelsea felt that her explanation had bounced off him without leaving a dent in his convictions.

Helen appeared in the doorway, her hand on Burke's arm. 'After sitting so long, I need help getting out of my chair,' she said, smiling. 'It's the price one pays for getting older.'

The sheer bravery of the woman took Chelsea's breath away. She was obviously in pain, but never would Helen admit that there was anything seriously wrong with her. 'I don't want sympathy,' she had told Chelsea once, in a rare confiding moment. 'I don't want people hovering over me, and watching out for what they say. I hate being an object of pity.'

And she never would be, Chelsea thought. When her time came, Helen Marshall would die as she had lived—proudly and self-sufficiently. And the world would be a worse place without her.

'Chelsea,' Helen said softly, 'there's a bottle of capsules on the table beside my bed. If you would bring me one . . .'

'Of course.' Chelsea ran up the stairs and stopped in the doorway of Helen's room. The pink and gold furnishings were the same as they had always been, except that where Helen's four-poster had stood was now a hospital bed, the electric variety that adjusted to any position. It was a jarring note in the princess-pretty room, and Chelsea went back downstairs in a sombre mood.

Nick was waiting impatiently to hold her chair. She dropped the capsule into Helen's hand and walked around the table to her own chair. 'It's so rare to find a gentleman these days,' Chelsea said with a sultry smile as Nick sat down beside her. And you aren't one, the tone of her voice added.

'Don't bait me, Miss Ryan,' he said so softly that she didn't think either Burke or Helen heard. 'You might not like the results.'

'Why, Mr Stanton,' she replied, and hated herself for sounding like a bad imitation of a Southern belle, 'can't a girl pay a man a compliment these days?'

'Knock it off,' Burke commanded. 'If I hear another Mister or Miss at this dinner table tonight I will send you both to your rooms.'

'Yes, Burke,' Chelsea said demurely and picked up her spoon.

So they were polite all through dinner, but underneath the courtesy was a vicious wit. And as she sipped clear consommé and nibbled at stuffed veal and crisp fresh vegetables and excellent hot rolls, Chelsea wondered why the venom was so hard to restrain. She knew why she didn't like Nick Stanton. But Nick had the job he wanted; why should he be angry at her?

Helen pleaded exhaustion, looking as if the pain of admitting that she could not brave out another hour of polite conversation hurt her even worse than her spine did. Burke helped her up the stairs, while Nick and Chelsea waited silently in the drawing room with the coffee tray for his return.

Chelsea hoped that he would take the hint and leave soon. She wanted to talk to Burke about the plans that were already underway for the new house. But Nick seemed to be very comfortable. He leaned back in his chair, looked up at the excellent oil portrait of Helen that hung above the fireplace, and said, 'What exactly did you do to this house?'

'Is that polite conversation or do you really want to know?' Chelsea refilled her delicate china cup from the huge silver pot.

He sat up slowly. 'If I didn't want to know, why would I ask?'

Chelsea shrugged. 'I'd guess that you merely want to criticise my architectural style. But I really don't care what you think. You see,' she added gently, 'I don't attempt to read a man's mind unless I'm interested in him.'

He looked her over with insulting thoroughness and then said, 'Of course, with Burke in the palm of your hand you wouldn't need to be interested in anyone else.'

'If you're implying that Burke's interest in me has had anything to do with my career . . .'

'I don't imply things, Miss Ryan,' he said with sardonic emphasis on the title. 'I come straight out and say them. I'm amazed that you aren't trying to fix an interest with me. Obviously Burke wasn't quite powerful enough, and yet you seem very loyal to him.'

Chelsea sat up very straight. 'It has nothing to do with . . .'

He cut her off neatly. 'Or are you after bigger game? Carl Shelby himself perhaps? Or Frank Harris?' Before Chelsea had regained her breath, Nick had changed the subject. 'You must have had quite a time replacing that cast plaster ceiling. It can't have been that way before, if this room was originally several small ones.'

'Don't remind me,' Burke said heartily from the door. 'We searched for months for an artisan who could do that work. Helen's poured a fortune into the place over the years, you know. You should see the pictures.'

Chelsea set her cup down firmly. 'Burke, it's been lovely——' Her voice sounded hollow to her own ears, and on Nick's face was the first smile she had ever seen there. 'But I'm tired. I'll see you at the office Monday—I have some plans to show you.' She retrieved her handbag and then stood on tiptoe to kiss Burke's cheek lightly.

Nick rose lazily. 'I'll walk you to your car. I should be on my way too, Burke.'

Outside the range of Hillhaven's lights, Chelsea turned on him fiercely. 'You needn't protect me, you know. I can walk to my car by myself.'

'Who said I was protecting you? As a matter of fact, I feel sorry for the attacker who takes you on.'

'You knew I wanted to talk to Burke privately . . .'

'I certainly did. And it didn't take a great deal of imagination to know what you were going to talk about. I simply refused to be a part of it.'

'What do you mean?' Chelsea stopped suddenly, in the middle of the street. 'You refused to be a part of what?'

He laughed sardonically. 'For all I know, you'll drive around the block and go back in. I can hardly stop you.'

Chelsea's head was spinning. 'And why shouldn't I go back to talk to Burke?' She stopped beside her car and took her keys from her handbag.

'A Mercedes,' he mused. 'I should have know.'

'It was a gift,' she flared, sensitive to the accusation in his tone.

'I didn't think that you earned it. Unless it was for services rendered.' He leaned against the fender, his arms folded. 'Did Burke use his own money to buy it, or did he charge it to Helen? You have a lot of nerve to steal from the woman you're deceiving.'

Her throat was so tight she could hardly breathe. Stupid, she thought. Everything he had said all evening led to that single conclusion; it had been staring at her and she had missed it. 'I am not having an affair with Burke Marshall,' she said. Her voice was taut.

'About those plans you intend to show Burke on Monday,' Nick added pleasantly. 'I'd like to see them first.'

'Those plans have nothing to do with the office,' Chelsea snapped, and bit her tongue.

Nick smiled. 'Somehow I expected that,' he murmured.

Chelsea opened the car door. 'If you would have the decency to get off my car, I'd like to go home.'

He didn't seem to hear. 'I am the boss now, Chelsea,' he warned.

'What does it matter to you whether I'm having an affair?' she asked, her curiosity raging despite her best efforts to keep quiet. 'Even if it was true, which it isn't . . .'

He interrupted. 'Because as long as people like you are licenced to practise architecture, it cheapens the rest of us who have worked like hell to get to where we are. I didn't earn my licence in a bedroom, and I resent women who do.'

She slammed the car door, rolled the window down,

and said, 'Don't take it personally, Mr Stanton.' The motor roared to life.

He moved unhurriedly away from the fender and leaned in the window. 'I take women like you very personally, Chelsea. You'd better get used to it.'

CHAPTER THREE

AND why should it matter to me? That was the question that tormented Chelsea throughout the weekend. It was still bothering her on Monday morning as she drank her second cup of coffee, standing at the kitchen counter in their little apartment.

If Nick Stanton chose to believe that Burke's interest in her was more than fatherly, that was his problem. There was no point in trying to convince him; any effort on her part would look as if she was guilty. Besides, it wouldn't take long for him to realise that she had talent, despite what he thought. Which brought her back to the original question: Why did it matter what Nick Stanton thought?

Judy came out of her bedroom, sleepy-eyed, still wearing her oversized nightshirt. She yawned and reached for a mug. 'The first week of working the evening shift is a drag,' she moaned. 'No social life and no sleep. Are you going to work already?'

'I left a lot of things hanging on Friday.'

'Trying to impress the new partner by going in early?' Judy guessed shrewdly.

'No? I told you what I think of him.'

'And what he thinks of you.' Judy dropped into a chair at the table and looked Chelsea over. 'I think it's funny. The idea of you and Burke as a twosome is laughable.'

'Too bad Nick doesn't see the humour.'

'I know what you should do. Invite him over for dinner.'

'I don't want to spend any more time with that . . . that cannibal than I absolutely must. Why should I see him on my own time?'

'Because if he saw where you live he'd know that this isn't any love nest of Burke Marshall's. That's why.'

Chelsea had to laugh. She looked around at the small kitchen. 'I've been meaning to talk to you. Don't you think we could afford to move?'

Judy shook her head. 'You can. I can't. Besides, there's a little reverse snob appeal in living here.'

'But it's more than half-an-hour from downtown.' Chelsea looked at her watch and hastily swallowed her coffee. 'Which means I'd better be going.'

'Hey, let's have lunch sometime this week, all right? Otherwise we won't see each other at all. I don't plan to be up at this hour every morning, you know, when I work till midnight.'

'Call me at the office.' Chelsea rinsed her cup.

Judy grinned. 'Which days do you reserve for Burke? I wouldn't want to interfere.'

Chelsea turned, the dripping mug in her hand, and threatened, 'You start on me and I'll move out.'

Which wouldn't be a bad idea at all, she thought as she threaded the Mercedes through heavy morning traffic on the Daniel Boone Expressway. She and Judy had shared an apartment for nearly five years. Before that there had been a succession of roommates since she had left home. Chelsea had never lived by herself, and it was beginning to look like an inviting idea. She could afford a nicer apartment now, which was more than she could have said five years before. And the cheap, boxy construction of their present home was beginning to wear on her artistic soul. She longed for some outstanding feature, something that would make her home different from the others.

Like Hillhaven, she thought, and then reluctantly put the idea aside. Even if Helen agreed to move, even if the house was sold, even if Chelsea could scrape up the mortgage payments, the maintenance and upkeep would impoverish her. She'd forgotten just how large a fortune Helen Marshall had poured into that house. No, Hillhaven was just a dream.

The man at the parking ramp waved as she took the time-punched ticket from the machine, and Chelsea smiled back, an every-morning routine. They ought to have a lottery with these tickets, she thought. Paying the bill in a parking ramp day after day was a dreary experience. But if the ticket number might be the lucky one to win a prize it would at least add a bit of excitement to the routine.

She crossed the skywalk and took the lift to the Shelby Harris floor. As she passed the closed walnut door of Nick Stanton's new office, she had to fight off an impulse to childishly stick out her tongue at the engraved nameplate. She didn't; she smiled ruefully at herself and walked on down the hall to her own office.

The office suite was quiet, the time of day when Chelsea did her best work. She got out the folder full of notes about the Sullivan's house, and started to work. She hadn't seen the site yet; that would be a project for this afternoon. She made it a habit never to begin to visualise a house until she had seen where it would stand. But in the meantime she could list the Sullivan's requirements and make sure her notes to herself were clear. A big workshop for Charles, a craft and hobby room for Doris—Chelsea wondered briefly just what sort of crafts she did. She probably crocheted rugs out of plastic bags, Chelsea thought dryly, and then brought herself back with a snap to the work at hand.

When Marie came in, Chelsea gave her a list of clients to contact. It was unusual for her to have so many projects on her desk at the same time; it seemed that half of St Louis was suddenly ready to build, and they all wanted Chelsea Ryan designs. Even Martin's clients seemed to be content to have Chelsea working for them instead. It was flattering, she thought, but she wondered what would happen if all twelve projects reached the construction stage at the same time. She'd be running all over greater St Louis every day trying to keep up with contractors.

She picked up the set of preliminary sketches for another house and started for Jim's office. Thank heaven for a draughtsman who knew what he was doing, she thought. Having Jim around had saved her hours of tedious drawing when it was time to turn the rough schematics into detailed floor plans.

'Hello, Jimmy-boy,' she sang out as she breezed into his office. 'Do I have a project for you. You're going to love this one.'

Nick Stanton turned from the draughting table and looked her over coolly from head to toe. 'I can hardly wait,' he drawled.

Chelsea couldn't help it; she went beetroot red and then pale as a ghost. 'Have they demoted you to draughtsman already?' she asked sweetly. 'I never dreamed the partners would catch on to you so quickly.'

'Your . . . friend . . .' The word was heavy with insinuation '. . . called in sick today. I was looking for the template I need when I ran across his unusual hobby.'

For the first time Chelsea saw what was scattered over the tabletop. In his right hand Nick held a sheet of draughting paper on which she could see the outline of Mount Rushmore, complete with four President's faces, and Nick's.

Chelsea started to feel a little ill. Dammit, she thought, Jim had promised to get those things out of the office.

'He had quite a lot of talent,' Nick said, holding up a sketch of Chelsea as an angel, halo slightly askew and eyes mischievous. 'This one is particularly appropriate. He might find a job as a political cartoonist after he gets fired here.'

'Jim didn't draw them.' Her voice was faint. There

was no point in pretending innocence, anyway. Everyone in the office would recognise Chelsea's style.

'I beg your pardon?' He sat down on the high-backed stool at the draughting table.

'Jim didn't draw them. I did.'

Nick's left eyebrow raised. It made him look like the Devil incarnate, bargaining for her soul. Except right now there was no bargaining to be done. Chelsea could see few options. 'Protecting Jim? Is he another of your lovers?'

'Jim is a friend and nothing more.'

'I doubt Burke would be convinced,' he drawled. 'You are really taking a risk for Jim, you know, Chelsea. If Burke finds out . . .'

'I'm telling the truth. My initials are on those sketches. See?'

He made a show of looking. 'Sorry, I don't see anything that marks them as yours.'

'I don't exactly advertise that I drew them!' Chelsea snapped. Reluctantly she walked towards him, holding out her hand for one of the drawings.

He didn't seem to see her. He held the drawing up to the light and inspected it. When Chelsea tried to snatch it out of his hand, Nick held it even higher and gave her a chiding look. 'Now, now,' he said. 'It won't do you any good to tear it up.' Leaning against the draughting stool as he was, he was still inches taller than she. Never before had Chelsea so regretted her lack of height.

'I didn't intend to destroy it. I was going to show you my initials.'

'Proud of your work?' he asked, and his eyes narrowed.

'Why shouldn't I be? You obviously think they're good, or you wouldn't be so angry.'

'And of course you're protecting your friend.'

'It's not fair to let him be blamed. I'm responsible.'

'So show me,' he said softly.

Chelsea looked thoughtfully from his face to the sketch. She would have to reach as high as she could just to put a finger on the paper. 'Give it to me.'

He shook his head. 'No way will I let you have this. Come here.'

It was a momentary battle of wills as their eyes locked. Chelsea gave in first and reluctantly stepped closer. By the time she could put her finger on the tiny monogram she had sketched into Abe Lincoln's beard, she was so close to Nick that she could feel his breath warm against her cheek. She felt trapped.

'So they are really yours. What's the matter? You aren't nervous, are you Chelsea?' he asked. His voice was very soft, but she wasn't fooled. Underneath the gentleness was a thread of steel.

'My name, as far as you are concerned, is Miss Ryan,' she said. Her voice shook just a tiny bit, and he smiled.

'Not any more,' he said softly. 'I'm tired of that game. Let's start a new one. I'm sure we have all sorts of things in common.' His fingertip traced the line of her chin.

'No, thanks.' Chelsea started to edge away from him, but his hand shot out and caught her elbow, holding her next to him in what was almost an embrace.

'It might be a lot of fun. But of course if you don't want to play——' His long slim hand fanned the sketches out on the drawing board and selected the one of Carl Shelby peering down Eileen's neckline. 'Carl might be very interested in seeing this one of him.'

'So show it to him.' Chelsea was damned if she'd submit to blackmail.

'You don't seem to understand the consequences,' Nick observed.

'If you don't give up these tactics, I'll file a complaint against you for sexual harrassment. And we'll see who comes out ahead.'

'I will,' he said. He didn't sound interested. 'I'm the fair-haired boy around here at the moment.'

'I shouldn't expect it to last long,' Chelsea snapped.

'Oh, I don't know.' His blue eyes, which had been icy, warmed. 'Do you think of every man in sexual terms, Chelsea? Or should I be flattered that you find me more attractive than most?' His fingertips slid gently down the silky sleeve to her delicate wrist.

'Attraction has nothing to do with it. Take your hand off me, you lecher! I don't care if you're the boss. I don't have to put up with this kind of nonsense!'

He ignored her request. 'Come to that, you could steam up a few windows yourself,' he said thoughtfully. 'Well, I'll give you a few days to think it over. It would be a shame to push you into a choice like that.'

'I don't play by those kind of rules,' Chelsea snapped. She pulled away from him.

He shrugged and turned away, pushing the caricatures into a careful stack. 'It seems to me you wrote the rules,' he said pleasantly.

'I'm a damn good architect, Mr Stanton,' she said. Her voice was trembling with anger.

'So you keep telling me. You have one chance to prove it. In the meantime, don't worry about your drawings. I'll keep them very, very safe.' He looked up then, his eyes brilliant. 'That's a promise, Chelsea.'

Marie cradled her telephone and handed Chelsea her appointment book. 'I contacted every one of those clients,' she said. 'It must be some sort of record to get them all in a single morning.'

Chelsea flipped through the book. 'I'll be stuck in the office for the next two weeks,' she complained. 'Any calls?'

'Just your mother. And there is a full staff meeting at one.'

'I was going out to the sites this afternoon,' Chelsea

muttered. Oh, well, overtime was part of the business, and she was certainly putting in her share. She just hoped that she could get to the Sullivan's lot before dark. 'Order me a sandwich from the deli downstairs, would you, Marie? I'll work through lunch.'

She dialled her parents' number and sketched a perspective drawing of a dressing room as she listened to the mysterious clickings and buzzings while her call worked its way upstate. Chelsea was no fool, but the intricacies of the telephone system defeated her. How a string of eleven digits could make a phone ring in a specific kitchen two hundred miles away was something she had never understood.

Her mother was cheerful. 'Hello, darling. Your father asked me to call you.'

'Oh?' Chelsea teased. 'Does that mean you didn't want to talk to me?' She began to shade in her drawing.

'Don't be difficult, dear. After all, telephones work both ways, and you could come home for a weekend now and then. Of course, I'm not trying to make you feel guilty.' But Sara Ryan's tone was light.

'It's been hectic around here for three months.'

'That's why Josh asked me to call. He'd like to take you to dinner Wednesday, and he wanted to be certain you could come.'

'I'll check my calendar,' Chelsea said in her best sophisticated tone. Then she started to laugh. 'I'd break any date I had to have dinner with Dad, and he knows it. What's the occasion?'

There was a long moment of silence. Then her mother said gently. 'It's your birthday, Chelsea.'

'I'd forgotten.'

'Chelsea? Are you certain you're feeling all right?'

'I think it's just that I'm getting a little older, Mom. Birthdays aren't as much fun these days.'

'It took me that way, too,' Sara said pensively.

'Why don't you come with him? We can celebrate

together.' Would she dare to ask for a day off right now, with all the work that was piled up on her desk? Nick Stanton would have fun with that request.

'Josh is coming on business.'

'Oh, now we get the truth. I'm not his very best girlfriend after all.'

Sara didn't bother to answer that one. 'I'd be bored to tears while he's in court.'

'Bring your easel and you can sit down on the riverbank and paint the Arch, or something.'

'That's hardly my style. Next time I'll come along and we'll go shopping—we'll buy you some new clothes.'

'I have a closetful now.'

Chelsea could almost see her mother's careless shrug. So what? she seemed to be saying. Sara Ryan had once been a clothing buyer for one of the big chain stores, and she had never got rid of the urge to dress Chelsea like a doll. Her taste was marvellous, too, but Chelsea suffered pangs of guilt every time Sara went on a shopping spree. She'd seen her mother shop, and she knew first hand that Sara never looked at a price tag.

'Thanks for the new green dress, by the way.'

'I'd almost forgotten sending you that one. Silly of me, isn't it?' Sara didn't sound worried. 'By the way, one of your old classmates called last week. He wanted to invite you to a barbecue the last weekend of May. A lot of your old friends will be back to visit.' Sara's tone was just a touch plaintive.

'I'll try to get up to Norah Springs soon, Mom.' It had been a long time since she'd been home. 'It depends on how many of these houses get off the drawing board and into construction. If my clients don't make some decisions soon, I'll still have a dozen projects next fall.'

'Surely it isn't necessary to work all the time,' Sara scolded.

'Right now it's a very good idea. I have a new boss, by the way.'

'Oh, Chelsea! You didn't get the partnership?'

''Fraid not, Mom. A woman in the higher echelons was just a little more than the partners could stand right now.'

'I was so certain you'd get it.'

'So was I,' Chelsea admitted. 'I'd better get back to work, Mom.'

'Is he nice?'

'Who? The new boss?' Nick Stanton's unsmiling face seemed to appear before her eyes, and Chelsea shuddered. 'No. See you later, Mom.'

She cradled the 'phone with a pang of loneliness. Chelsea was that rare person who had come to adulthood as a true good friend of both her parents. Given the choice, she was delighted to spend time with them. But since she had moved to St Louis, her time at home was rare.

It was an option, though. If life at Shelby Harris became unbearable . . . 'No, Chelsea,' she told herself firmly. 'Be honest. It's Nick Stanton that might become unbearable. And you could always go back to Norah Springs and open a practice of your own.'

Her parents would be delighted. For a moment, Chelsea sat there at the drawing board, staring out across the bustle of downtown St Louis and hearing instead the calm quiet of Norah Springs. Then her backbone straightened, and her little pointed chin set firmly. She was damned if Nick Stanton would drive her out of this firm and this city, and this job she had worked so hard to get. She would fight him, and she would win.

The staff meeting droned on until Chelsea was ready to scream. It was the one time of the week when all the partners and staff architects met to compare notes, and usually she was eager to find out what the other divisions of the practice were doing. But when her own desk was piled high, Chelsea's enthusiasm for discussion was lacking.

Plus, she had to admit, it wasn't pleasant to find herself sitting across the conference table from Nick, who was jotting occasional notes to himself on a legal pad and who seemed to spend most of his time looking through Chelsea.

She summarised the progress of her own projects and tried not to notice Nick's pen skimming down the legal pad as she talked. Was he ignoring her completely, she wondered, or were all those notes referring to her houses? If so, she was in trouble already, she thought grimly.

'Is that everything?' Carl Shelby asked finally. At the nods from around the table, Chelsea started to push her chair back. But Carl didn't stop talking. 'There is a new competition beginning this week, that I want to talk to you all about.'

Chelsea tried to hide her sigh and pulled her chair back to the table. At this rate she might as well sleep in the office tonight, she thought glumly.

'You all know the Jonas Building, of course. To refresh your memories, it was the downtown anchor of the department store chain. It was built at the turn of the century, and it was one of the biggest buildings in the city for years.'

'Eight stories, granite and brick construction, cast iron façade and columns,' Nick added quietly. He hadn't looked up from the notebook. 'Not a particularly important building.'

Chelsea happened to be looking at one of the apprentice architects at the time, and she nearly choked with laughter at the expression on his face. He looked as startled as if Nick had suddenly pulled a rabbit out of a hat. Calm down, she wanted to tell him. If Carl Shelby knew about a contest, all the partners did. Nick would have had plenty of time to do his research. It didn't mean that he knew every obscure building in St Louis!

'It's worth saving, none the less,' Frank Harris said, looking a little offended. 'Most of the cast iron architecture in the city has been destroyed. And it was one of our most important industries.'

'Of course it's worth saving. If it's properly done.' Nick's words were conciliating, but his tone didn't give an inch.

'The store has been closed about five years. With business shifting to the suburbs, it didn't pay the company to keep it open. They nearly tore it down a couple of years ago. Some of you probably remember.'

Chelsea did. Groups of people interested in preserving the city's past had picketed the store's headquarters till the management gave in.

'Then they tried to sell it, and had no luck with that,' Carl continued. 'Now the company is sponsoring a contest for the best plans to re-model the building. Their idea is shops on the lower floors and condos on the top.'

Nick was doodling now, Chelsea saw. 'Office space?' he asked.

Shelby shook his head. 'No offices—their marketing research says there is no demand in the downtown area at present.' He leaned forward and said in a confiding tone, 'I don't mind telling you all I want this firm to win that competition. We'll submit one entry from this office, and we'll win the prize, because Shelby Harris is the best in the business. I have the details, specs, and blueprints in my office for all of you who want to take it on.'

He pushed his chair back from the table. 'Don't waste any time, though,' he warned. 'They're in a hurry for this, and the deadline is not far off. If there is nothing else to discuss, we'll meet again next week.'

Chelsea tried to vanish silently, but Burke stopped

her by the door. 'Didn't you say you have something to show me?' he asked.

She could feel Nick's gaze on the nape of her neck. 'I'd rather talk about it after office hours, Burke.' The designs for the new house were strictly free-lance; they had nothing to do with the firm, and so they were none of Nick's business. And she knew that Burke would rather no one else knew about them, either, at least till Helen had given her blessing.

He looked puzzled, but agreed. 'Then I'll buy you a drink after work.'

'Sorry, Burke. I don't know where I'll be at quitting time. I'm on my way out to the sites now.'

'All right. Perhaps tomorrow then. By the way, a neighbour of ours down the block wants to renovate his house. It's quite similar to Hillhaven—I told him about your work.'

Chelsea groaned. 'That's all I need right now, Burke—another project!'

'Well, he'll give you a call anyway.'

Chelsea started for her office, but Nick caught her in the hall. 'I'll meet you in my office in ten minutes,' he said. 'Bring all the designs you're working on at the moment.'

Chelsea looked up at him coldly. 'I've planned my afternoon, Mr Stanton. I have two houses to stake out and a new lot to look over. I have no time to discuss my work.'

'Make time,' he recommended, and turned away.

'It would be easier to move you than it is to bring all my designs. If you want to see them, you can come to my office,' she snapped.

He didn't appear to have heard, and Chelsea went back to her own office feeling grim. Norah Springs and a little office next to her father's law pracitce was sounding better and better, she thought resentfully.

She was just putting on her hat when Nick walked

in. 'Knocking is still considered good manners,' she snapped.

'Sorry. I didn't stop to think about what I might find here,' he said cheerfully and sat down on the corner of her desk, arms folded. 'You're absolutely right.'

Somehow she didn't feel as if she'd won anything. 'If you'll excuse me, I really haven't time to go over all my current projects this afternoon.'

'I believe you said that before,' he said. 'Go ahead, if you must leave. I'll just look at them by myself.' He leaned over the drawing board and unrolled a set of blueprints.

Chelsea sighed and put her hat back in the closet. She couldn't just leave him there with her precious drawings; he might do anything. 'That's the Emerson house,' she said.

Nick looked up with a glint in his eyes. 'I can read,' he said gently.

'You amaze me. Anything you want to know?'

'No. I think it's all here.' He scanned the blueprints with a practised eye and laid them aside.

'I'm staking that one out this afternoon,' she said. 'Unless, of course, you want to do it over?'

'No, thanks. Houses really aren't my line.'

'They don't seem to appeal to anyone around this practice, except me,' Chelsea muttered. 'Martin liked them, but no one else does.'

'And you inherited his unfinished work.'

'Yes, and all of his clients have been very pleased, too,' she snapped.

He didn't answer. He just loosened his tie, pulled a stool up to the drawing board, and started to work. In half an hour he had inspected every drawing, every preliminary sketch, every construction document, right down to the casual notes for the Sullivan house. As he laid those aside, he leaned back against the drawing board, tapped his pencil thoughtfully against the edge, and studied her with a speculative gleam in his eyes. 'I don't see anything for Burke,' he commented.

'And you won't either,' Chelsea retorted, before she had a chance to think how foolish an answer it was.

'That means that I was right—your plans didn't have anything to do with architecture. I must say it doesn't surprise me. What does amaze me is that you had the sense to keep it out of the office today. You may be learning after all, Chelsea.'

She didn't bother to answer that one. 'If you've finished, I'd like to go stake out those houses so the contractors can start this week.'

'Let me get my jacket.'

'Why do you need your . . . Hey, I don't want your help.'

Nick's eyebrows raised. 'Who asked if you wanted help? I'm just doing a little field research—catching up with the projects that are under my direction.'

'Don't you have any of your own to work on?'

'Not yet,' he said pleasantly. 'I didn't bring a single commission with me. So you can count on me for any assistance you need. I'll be right at your elbow all the time, at least till my own practice builds up again.'

'I'm not an apprentice, you know. I'm a fully licenced architect and I can practise without anyone supervising me.'

'I know you can,' he said. 'But you aren't going to. Make up your mind to having me hanging around.'

'Why don't you just fire me outright, Nick?'

'Oh, I wouldn't do that,' he said. 'But I'm going to make sure you have plenty of opportunities to trip yourself up. The first mistake you make will be your last one at Shelby Harris, Chelsea.'

CHAPTER FOUR

THE roar of the Mercedes engine echoed in the parking ramp, and Chelsea sat for several seconds with her foot on the brake. She looked over at Nick finally and said, 'Are you certain you don't have anything you'd rather do this afternoon than help me stake out houses?'

'Can't think of a thing,' he said cheerfully. She sighed and put the car into gear.

The parking lot attendant turned his radio down when he saw the Mercedes coming. He leaned out of the window, popping his bubble gum in time to the music, to take the ticket and money out of Chelsea's hand. 'There you go, darlin',' he said cheerfully as he dropped the change into her palm.

'Darling?' Nick asked. 'Not him, too?'

Chelsea put her sunglasses on and tossed the change into her purse. 'Just how many affairs do you think I can manage at one time, anyway?' she asked tartly. 'I'm not Superwoman, and he calls everybody darling.' To get rid of some of her frustrations, she stepped on the accelerator a little harder than she otherwise would have, sending the Mercedes flying out on to the street.

Nick's head snapped back against the headrest. 'I hope you're insured for my whiplash,' he said.

'That's the risk you take when you force your company on me.'

'I'm just doing my job as your supervisor. And by the way, every plan that goes out of your office from now on must have my signature on it.'

Chelsea was so angry that she let the Mercedes drift across into the oncoming lane, and only pulled it back when another driver's horn blared.

'Do you plan to still have this car by the end of the

day?' Nick asked. 'If so, would you kindly pay attention to your driving?'

She ignored that. 'After my apprenticeship was over, Martin never again asked to see a line of my work. If I got into trouble, I took it to him, but . . .'

'Remember?' he interrupted. 'I'm not Martin.'

'In the four years I've been at Shelby Harris I have worked on a couple of hundred houses. I am damned if I'm going to . . .'

'Look on it as an opportunity to instruct me,' Nick said calmly. 'Just think how much I can learn from watching you work.'

She would have thrown something at him, but there was nothing close at hand. So Chelsea bit her lip and guided the car on to the expressway.

'Would you like to tell me about these projects?'

'No,' Chelsea said sweetly. 'You saw the blueprints. What else do you want?'

'What kind of house are you planning for the Sullivans?'

'How should I know? I haven't seen the lot, yet. We're going there first, by the way.'

'Let's drive by the Jonas Building on the way.'

She looked over at him curiously and then switched on the turn signal. 'Why don't you hire a chauffeur?'

'Because you're handy.'

She slowed the Mercedes to a crawl as they drove past the massive old building. 'You can almost see the buggies driving by on the granite streets, can't you?' she remarked.

'It certainly looks as if it hasn't had a facelift in eighty years,' Nick agreed absently. He was running a practised eye over the fluted cast iron columns that set off the first floor display windows.

Chelsea turned the corner. 'Look, there are french doors on the second floor,' she remarked. 'I don't remember those, and I've driven by that store a million times.'

'At least there's plenty of light to work with—all that cast iron framing is good for something.'

'Seen enough?'

'For right now. What's it like inside?'

'Nick, I haven't been in that store in twenty years, and I think then we were shopping for a teddy bear. There's a big central open area that goes all the way to the ceiling—with skylights, I think. I can't remember anything else. Are you going to submit a plan?'

He shrugged. 'Now tell me what you're going to design for the Sullivans,' he suggested. 'You have the site plans. Surely you have some ideas.'

'Oh, we aren't going to talk about the Jonas Building?' She took the Mercedes up the freeway ramp with a roar, and Nick winced..

'Site plans don't always tell the whole truth, you know,' she pointed out. 'And I make it a practise never to visualise a house until I see the land. It doesn't start to take shape in my mind till then.'

He didn't answer. 'While we're out, how about showing me some of the sights?'

'Are you going tourist on me? To your right in a few minutes you will have Forest Park, home of the zoo, the art museum and the municipal opera. That's about the size of the sights in this part of town.'

'You lack enthusiasm as a guide. Is it me, or don't you appreciate the attractions of your home town?'

'It isn't my home town. But I like the zoo and the opera just fine, and I get positively sentimental about the art museum.'

'Why? Did you meet Burke there?'

'No. But it would be a good enough reason.' They were silent until the Mercedes left the freeway and dropped down into the city again. 'There's a street map in the glovebox,' Chelsea said. 'Would you look for the turnoff, please?'

He hunted for the map. 'What would you do

without me?' he asked cheerfully.

'Pull off to the side and find it myself, thank you.'

'You really prefer to work alone, don't you Chelsea?'

'Yes. Design by committee usually results in trash. That's why I stick to houses; there is only room for me to work on them.'

'Was that supposed to give me a message?'

'It certainly was,' she said pleasantly.

There was a silence as Nick watched street signs. 'That was it, back there.'

'You could have warned me.' Chelsea wheeled the Mercedes into a driveway and backed out, heedless of oncoming traffic.

'Watch out for the . . .' He bit his tongue, and said, 'Are you going to work on the contest project?'

'I thought we weren't going to talk about the Jonas Building. Anyway, why would I want to?'

'Because it's a challenge.'

'I have plenty of challenges already. That big block-square barn holds no attraction for me. Even if I'd work on it, by the time Carl Shelby got done with my proposal, it wouldn't bear any resemblance to what I started with. Carl and I don't agree on much when it comes to architecture.'

'You and Burke obviously do,' he remarked.

'Burke's a little different.'

'He certainly seems to be. Especially where you're concerned.'

Chelsea didn't answer. She propped the site plan against the steering wheel and let the Mercedes creep up to the curb in front of the Sullivan's lot. 'That's the deepest ravine I've seen in years,' she said. 'If Doris Sullivan wants to live out in the wild, she certainly picked a good spot.' She shut the engine off, kicked off her shoes, and reached into the back seat for her pumps.

'It's going to take a lot of fill,' Nick said.

Chelsea looked up in surprise, but she couldn't tell whether he was serious. 'Why?'

'Because you can't build on air, that's why.'

She tied the shoe-strings thoughtfully. 'You are joking, aren't you? Or did you skip residential architecture altogether?' She didn't wait for an answer.

She wandered over the lot, studying it from the bottom of the ravine, from the top, from the lawn of the house next door. She stood there for a long time, eyes closed, visualising what the Sullivan's house should be. It was going to be tough, she thought. The house would have to be multi-level because of the site, and that was hardly ideal for a couple the age of the Sullivans.

Well, that isn't my problem, Chelsea decided. If they want to build in a ravine, they'll have to accept the drawbacks.

'What are you doing?' Nick asked.

She opened her eyes and gave him an exasperated stare. 'Look, you can force me to turn in all of my plans for your approval—whatever that's worth—but you can't make me share them before they're written down, for heaven's sake. Just leave me alone, would you?'

He did, wandering over the steep hillside with his hands deep in his pockets. He'd left his jacket in the car, and his blue shirt was a spot of distinctive colour among the yellow-green of spring. He stooped to pick up a branch, and Chelsea told herself firmly to stop watching Nick and concentrate on the house plans. She was beginning to see it now; a small but spacious house half buried in the side of the ravine . . .

'What are you doing?' The question was repeated, but this time it was a friendly voice at her elbow.

Chelsea looked down to find a freckled, chubby-cheeked little girl, her blonde hair tied up in pigtails, beside her. She was probably four years old, Chelsea thought.

'I'm just looking at the land. We're going to build a house down there this summer.'

The child looked delighted. 'A whole new house?'

Chelsea laughed. 'Brand new.'

A warm little hand was tucked confidingly into hers. 'What's it going to look like?'

'I don't know yet. That's what I'm thinking about now.'

The child turned that over in her mind for a moment. 'Do you have any little girls like me?'

'What? Oh, the house isn't for me, honey. I'm the architect, but I won't be living here.'

'Oh.' The child's face dropped, and Chelsea almost felt guilty that she wasn't the new owner.

You're losing your touch, Chelsea, she told herself. A four-year-old smiles at you, and you become a marshmallow.

They were on the way to the next site before Nick said, 'I see you found a friend back there.'

Chelsea shrugged. 'She thought I was going to be her new neighbour.'

'You charm them from the cradle to the grave, don't you?' he asked, with admiration in his voice. 'So tell me. What is the Sullivan's house going to look like?'

'What makes you think that I know?' Chelsea countered.

'Because you'd have stood there all night if necessary, till you saw it. As soon as you did, you relaxed.'

It bothered her, that he had read her mood so easily. Obviously he'd been watching her more closely than she had thought.

'Tell you what,' she offered suddenly. 'I'll make you a little bet.'

'I'm listening.'

'What if you design the Sullivan's house, too, and we show both plans to a neutral party? If yours is better than mine, I'll submit everything I draw from now on for your approval without a whimper. But if mine is better, then I can go back to working on my own—no interference.'

Nick shrugged. 'You're on. You won't win, of course. It's not a very sensible bet to make, you know.'

'What have I got to lose?' Chelsea countered.

He smiled, and drawled, 'You might be surprised.'

The Mississippi River washed gently against the old brick levee, and across the warm night air came whispers of Dixieland jazz. Chelsea's high-heeled sandal tapped impatiently on the gangway as she and her father boarded the riverboat restaurant, and Josh Ryan laughed. 'Chelsea, you'll fall overboard if you keep that up,' he warned.

'I can't help it. My feet just won't stay still when I hear Dixieland.'

He had turned to the hostess on the main deck. 'We have reservations for Ryan.'

'The first dinner seating,' the hostess commented. 'You're right on time, Mr Ryan. Your table is ready on the steak deck, to your right, if you'd like to go on in. And welcome aboard!'

'Daddy,' Chelsea protested. 'You know how much I like the lounge. Can't we go listen to the music?'

'After dinner,' he said firmly. 'Chelsea, have a heart. I've been in court all day, and I'm starving.'

Chelsea relented. He held her chair and then dropped into one across from her. For the first time she realised how tired he looked. 'How is the case going?'

He shook his head. 'It's over. But sometimes I wish appeals courts had never been invented.'

'Especially when you won the original case, right?'

A reluctant grin reached his eyes. 'Exactly. I'm representing George Bradley again.'

'My favourite tycoon?'

'Is there another one? We won the case hands down at the first trial, but who knows what the court will say this time? The appeals could drag on for years.' He stared moodily into his water glass. 'But let's find a happier subject for your birthday dinner, all right?'

Above them, the steam whistle blew, and the riverboat glided into motion on its way downriver for the dinner cruise. Chelsea looked out at the darkening shoreline. 'This is my very favourite place to eat, you know.'

'I know. Darn your mother—she had to raise you to be a romantic just like her.'

'And you had nothing to do with it, I know,' Chelsea teased gently.

'Who, me?' He sounded astonished. 'All I did was propose to her on the art museum lawn at midnight. Fillet or prime rib, Chelsea?'

'Oh, the rib, of course. Rare.'

'And champagne, to make up for missing the lounge?'

Chelsea laughed. 'The champagne doesn't have the same atmosphere. Now if they delivered it with a Dixieland . . .'

'Listen closely and you can hear the one in the lounge,' he recommended. 'How does it feel to be twenty-seven?'

She grimaced. 'Not as good as nineteen, but since I don't have an option, I'll just have to get used to it.'

He gave their order to the waiter. 'Your mother said the partnership fell through.'

'Ouch. I thought you said something about happy topics.' Chelsea handed her menu over.

'So instead of being the boss, you have a new one.'

'That's right. Tell me, can a good architect make a living in Norah Springs these days?'

'That bad, hmmm?'

'Oh, Nick Stanton is excellent, especially on big projects—office buildings, that sort of thing. He's done a couple of beautiful skyscrapers. But he's impossible to work with. He's somehow got the idea that ...' She had second thoughts about telling her father about Nick's crazy suspicions about Burke, and stopped there. 'You've had personality clashes sometimes, haven't you, Dad? I mean, two people can both be perfectly reasonable, but they still can't get along together.' Not that Nick Stanton is reasonable, she thought, but the principle applies.

'It happens. I've had a lot of cases through the years that could have been settled amicably if the people hadn't hated each other to begin with. Are you serious about coming home?'

'I don't know just now. It depends on how bad it gets at Shelby Harris. I can't imagine getting rich by building two houses a year in Norah Springs. And to do that I'd have to get the commissions on all the new construction!'

Josh shrugged. 'You did a good job with Bradley's house. He told me that they're always getting comments about it.'

Chelsea sipped the champagne the waiter poured for her and murmured. 'Probably a lot of remarks about him going clear to St Louis for a high-falutin' architect.'

'Well, some of that too,' her father admitted. 'It would make a good advertisement for you, though, if you decide to hang out a shingle. And then there is our house, of course— though some people think we're prejudiced when we tell them how much we love it.'

'Building the Bradley house was fun,' Chelsea mused. 'Working within strict limits is a challenge, but it was delightful to have no budget restraints for once.' She smiled, reminiscently.

'In any case, you don't need to worry about the money, dear. If you come back to Norah Springs, your mother and I will see that you don't starve.'

'I would probably need some help,' Chelsea

admitted. 'But Dad, you know that I want to be independent. I don't like to take money from you and Mom. It's bad enough that she sends me clothes every other week.'

'I don't understand why you're so sensitive about it. You're our only child, Chelsea, and there is no point in you scrimping and saving on your own and then paying inheritance tax when we're gone.'

She shook a finger at him. 'Dad, you're far too young to be thinking about things like inheritance tax.'

'An attorney who doesn't think of things like that is a fool.'

'I don't care if you write your darn will, but don't talk to me about it, all right?' She sat back in her chair and stared at him, her chin defiant. If it wasn't for the streak of white hair at each temple, Josh Ryan could pass for forty. And he took excellent care of himself. In winter it was handball and swimming, in summer tennis and golf. He was still as trim in dinner clothes as he had appeared in his wedding pictures; he said it gave him an advantage in the courtroom to look better than his opponents. 'If there ever was a candidate to reach the age of a hundred, it's you, Dad. So stop trying to make me feel sorry for you.'

'You win. But I'd like to point out, Chelsea, that I didn't hear anything about independence when we bought that sporty little car of yours.'

'That was a gift, Dad. It was completely different.'

'If you say so, Chelsea.' He raised his glass. 'To my lovely daughter, who makes twenty-seven look wonderful.'

'Thank, Dad.' She was a little misty-eyed as they touched glasses, and she was thoughtful as she sipped the tangy wine. Her father was a darling, and if things didn't get better she might take him up on that offer. If she could just have that little office rent-free for a few months, she was certain that she could make it work.

She looked up from her glass, and her eye was caught by a dark-haired man at a table across the room. He was alone, and he looked like . . .

'Oh, my God,' she said as Nick raised his glass in an ironic salute. What awful luck had brought him here, on this evening-long cruise, she wondered?

Her father had bent over to rummage in his attaché case. 'What did you say?'

'Oh—nothing.'

He didn't push the subject. Instead he set a box before her. It was small and nearly square, wrapped in silver paper, with a matching bow that—before it had been crushed in the attaché case—had been huge and elegant. 'Sorry about the ribbon,' he said. 'That's just a little something from your mother.'

Chelsea eyed the box with foreboding. 'I've had some experience with Mom's idea of a little something,' she said, and pleaded silently, please don't make me open it here. Not with Nick sitting over there watching.

'Go ahead,' her father invited. 'Rip it open. I don't even know what it is, but she told me it was something you'd really like. Just a little nonsense thing.'

Chelsea closed her eyes for a second and sent a silent prayer skyward. Please let Mother have exercised some sense this time, she thought. It wasn't that her mother's gifts were ever in bad taste. They were always elegant and lovely and well-chosen. It was just that they were also horribly expensive. If only this time Sara really had sent a nonsense gift!—something that she wouldn't mind unwrapping in front of Nick Stanton . . .

Think positive, Chelsea, she told herself. At least it's a smaller box than last year's, so it can't be another bronze sculpture.

She unwrapped the box gingerly, as if expecting it to bite her. The name of the store did nothing to soothe her anxiety, for it was Sara's favourite jewellery store. Chelsea pulled open the box and took out a tissue wrapped bundle.

'A coffee mug?' she asked as the tissue slid away from the handle. But her instant of relief passed as she took the rest of the paper off. The mug was heavy in her hand, and she didn't have to look at the small, distinctive green label, or the equally obvious facets in the glass to know she was holding a piece of hand-blown, hand-cut crystal.

'A Waterford crystal mug?' she asked. 'What in the world does she expect me to drink out of a crystal mug?'

Josh shrugged. 'Champagne, I suppose. Would you care for some more?'

'No, thanks, I wouldn't dare put hot coffee in it,' Chelsea mused, and wrapped it carefully again.

'That must be why your mother said it was a silly thing.'

'Only Mom would consider a piece of hand-cut crystal a gag gift.'

'Though come to think of it, I don't know why it wouldn't work for coffee. In fact, it would be kind of pretty.'

'I'll think about it.' Chelsea laid it carefully back in the box, and just then the waiter served their meal. She was very careful not to look over towards Nick's table again; she didn't want to see the expression on his face. With her luck, he'd turn out to be a connoisseur of Waterford crystal.

The whole upper deck was devoted to the lounge, where most passengers spent the majority of the cruise. The Dixieland band was playing 'St Louis Blues' as Chelsea found her way to a table in the open section on the forward deck. 'This should be just right,' she said as Josh pulled out her chair. 'It's far enough from the music so that it isn't deafening.'

The cool river air brushed her face and made her glad of the lacy shawl that lay about her shoulders over the pastel lilac dress. The deck was dimly lit, with lamps on each table casting a dull glow. When viewed from the shore, Chelsea knew, the riverboat was rimmed with brilliant lights and looked almost as if there was a carnival on the river. But on board, the atmosphere was dim and intimate, a retreat for lovers.

She sipped her pina colada and thought about it. Here she was, on a riverboat meant for lovers, with her father. Birthdays were a time for taking stock, and perhaps at twenty-seven it was time for her to do that. 'Perhaps I'm ready for a change,' she mused.

'Coming home, and setting up your own practice?'

Chelsea nodded. 'That's one possibility. I was thinking about moving, too. Even if I stay here in the city, I mean. Judy is a good friend, but . . .'

Josh swirled his drink and set it down. 'Do you want a place of your own, or do you have another roommate lined up?'

She smiled, and her face lighted. 'A man, do you mean?'

'It has crossed my mind,' Josh said gently.

'Would you be upset?' she asked curiously.

He shrugged. 'Depends on the man. But I imagine you would be careful with your choice.'

'I should hope so. There really isn't anybody in my life right now. Does that disappoint you, Daddy?'

'Me? Disappointed that my daughter might be a spinster?' Mock horror dripped from the word.

'Only because I haven't found anybody like you. Mom was lucky, you know. You both were.' Her voice was pensive. Then, suddenly, she smiled and patted his hand. 'When I find a man like you, Dad, then you can walk me down the aisle.'

'That's gratifying. Misguided, perhaps, but gratifying. Let's take a turn around the deck.

'Why is it misguided to look for someone like you?' she questioned as they stood at the back rail, watching the huge paddle revolve as the boat made its wide sweeping turn and began to churn its way back upriver.

'Because you don't need a man just like me. And if you could find one, you'd discover that you didn't really want him, either. You're not like your mother, dear. Her dream man——' he bowed—'is not yours.'

Chelsea laughed. 'So what should I be looking for?'

He looked down at her, and Chelsea could feel the gentleness of his smile. 'Only you can know that, Chelsea. And if you don't find it—well, there are worse things than being alone. Some of the divorces I've worked on are enough to sour anyone to the state of matrimony. My God, those people should have never married.'

Chelsea turned to look out over the river. 'Maybe they thought they loved each other.'

'And maybe they seized on what looked like the last opportunity to get married, too. Don't do that, Chelsea,' he said and his voice was stern. 'Don't marry at all unless you are sure you want him, and not just that wedding ring.'

She laughed. 'I'll keep that in mind. But if it doesn't work, I'm sure you'd give me a cut rate on a divorce.'

'Chelsea, I'm going to shake you!' he threatened. 'That's exactly the attitude that worries me about young people getting married today—they walk to the altar thinking that if it doesn't work they'll just get a divorce. A lot of your school friends are already on marriage number two, and . . .'

Chelsea interrupted, suddenly serious. 'You don't have to preach to me, Dad.'

'Sorry.' He grinned sheepishly. 'I was, wasn't I?'

She nodded gently. 'If I can't find the same thing in marriage that you and Mom have, then I'd rather be alone.'

'Friendship. That's it in a word, you know. Your mother and I are best friends.'

'Then that's what I'll look for. Thanks, Dad.' She put her arm around his waist and they stood there for a long time, staring out over the river. Finally Josh patted her shoulder and said, 'I'm going after another drink. Want one?'

'No, thanks. One of those frothy things is my limit.' Chelsea's voice was dreamy as she looked out into the midnight blue.

'Then would you mind keeping an eye on my briefcase? I hate to carry it around.'

'Why didn't you just leave it at the hotel?'

'I am not a fool, Chelsea. Clothes and toothbrushes are replaceable, valuable papers are not. At least not by tomorrow morning. And I didn't have time to check it into the vault.'

'I thought you were finished in court today.'

'I was. I didn't say it contained court documents.'

'Oh. I thought George Bradley had retired. Is he working on another deal?'

'Sometimes, Chelsea, you are too darn telepathic for your own good,' he scolded and went off towards the bar.

She shook her head, smiling. Her father had neither confirmed her suspicion nor denied it, and he wouldn't. No wonder the old fox was such a good attorney, she thought.

'All alone in the dark?' A voice came out of the darkness, and Nick Stanton followed.

Chelsea turned her back to him. She'd actually forgotten that he was on board, she thought, and wished that she had trailed down the promenade to the bar with her father.

'This isn't a safe place to be alone,' he continued.

'Obviously,' she said, over her shoulder. 'Especially as long as there are wolves like you on board.'

'I'll stay around to protect you,' he said, and came over to the rail. 'I'm amazed that your companion would leave you up here.'

'He just went down for a drink.'

'Champagne and a gift at dinner, and then he leaves you alone on deck? It isn't very polite of him.'

'You needn't stick around. In fact, please get lost, Nick.' She stared out over the dark water.

'I thought perhaps you'd like to introduce me.' His voice was caressingly soft, and his fingers brushed the delicate skin on her shoulder as he tucked the shawl closer about her.

Chelsea's spine straightened and she took a step away from him. 'Now why would I want to do that? And just what do I have to thank for the honour of finding you aboard?'

'Dinner cruises are such a good idea, aren't they?' he mused. 'Especially when one is trying to hide out. It makes it much less of a risk than the average restaurant, where people keep coming and going. At the ordinary restaurant, you might even run into— Burke, or someone. And that would be very embarrassing. Or are you using this one to cover up your relationship with Burke?'

So he thought that her father was yet another lover. She'd never met anyone who was so suspicious. Well, Chelsea wasn't about to straighten him out; someday soon Nicholas Stanton was bound to make a fool of himself, and she would do nothing to prevent that happy day from arriving quickly.

'You were very discreet, to make the reservation in your own name. But it was not so discreet to mention it to your secretary this afternoon.' He took a step closer and raised a hand to her cheek, brushing back the tendrils of auburn hair that had been teased loose by the breeze.

'So you decided to come along.'

'It wasn't entirely because of you. I've been told that you haven't really seen St Louis till you view it from a riverboat.'

'That's true,' she said reluctantly, and then warmed

to the subject, hoping to distract him. 'From the water, you can see it the way the old settlers did, and almost ignore the new skyline.'

He didn't seem interested. 'I have to grant you better taste with this one,' he said thoughtfully. 'A whole lot younger than Burke; probably a great deal more fun. Just what do you stand to gain from him? Or is it just toys like the crystal mug?'

'I don't know why you think it's any of your business.'

Nick moved suddenly, putting a hand on the rail on each side of her, and Chelsea found herself trapped. 'Do you like pretty things, Chelsea?' he asked. 'You should. You are a pretty thing yourself.' His mouth was so close to hers that she could almost feel the shape of his words.

She turned suddenly away from him, clenching her hands on the rail to keep from hitting him. 'Go away, Nick.'

'Till later,' he said, and his hands were warm on her bare shoulders, sliding intimately under the shawl. 'That's a promise, Chelsea.'

He left so silently that she wasn't even sure for a time whether he was still there. When she finally looked around, a shudder of relief hit her as she realised that he was gone. A couple of minutes later her father came down the promenade.

'Sorry, dear, the bar was busy. I see we're almost home.'

Chelsea hadn't noticed. She looked up then at the sheen of moonlight on the stainless steel of the Gateway Arch, at the gleam of lights along the riverfront, at the dark bulk of the arched bridge that stretched across the Mississippi. She heard, dimly, the Dixieland band start to play 'Won't You Come Home, Bill Bailey?'

Home, she thought. Was going home the answer?

'Want me to keep that office open for a while, Chelsea?' her father asked. 'Just in case you want it?'

'You're a little telepathic yourself, you know,' she said. It would be so easy. She'd have to work at building up a practice, but it would be so nice not to have to fight . . .

Then that stubborn little jaw set. No matter how hard he tried, Nick Stanton was not going to drive her out. He might succeed in getting her fired, but he could not make her run.

'No, Dad,' she said, and her voice was steady. 'Rent it. I won't need it.'

CHAPTER FIVE

SHE was filling the crystal mug from the coffee machine in the employee's lounge the next morning when Nick came in. She saw, out of the corner of her eye, that his mouth tightened when he spotted the mug, and was insanely glad, deep inside, that she had given in to frivolous instinct and brought it to work.

'Good morning,' she said brightly, and tried to brush past him in the doorway. Confuse the enemy! that was her new strategy.

But he settled himself against the jamb and said, 'You're very cheerful this morning. Cruises must do you good.'

'Innuendo doesn't suit you,' she said, shaking her head sadly. 'You're much better with the direct approach.'

He just raised an eyebrow. 'Let me get my coffee and I'll be in to help you this morning.'

'With help like you, I could be six months doing this week's work,' Chelsea retorted.

She was at her drawing board, working on the preliminary sketches of the Sullivan house, when there was a tap on her door. She grimaced and scrambled the drawings into a drawer. The last thing she wanted was for Nick to see those sketches. After they were out of sight, she called, 'Come in.'

It was Jim, and he was pale. 'Chelsea—those caricatures. They're gone.'

'I know.'

He took a deep breath. 'You took them? Thank heaven. I know I promised to take them home, and I really meant to, but I forgot, and . . .'

'I don't have them. I simply know where they are, and it would take a bit of burglary to get them back. Nick Stanton has them.'

Jim's face darkened. 'We're done, Chelsea.'

'I don't know about you. He's using them to blackmail me.'

He just shook his head.

Chelsea picked up her pencil again. 'By the way, Jim, he'll be designing a house in the next week or so. The Sullivan house—but he may not call it that. It sits down in a ravine. When you get the drawings . . .'

Jim looked puzzled for an instant.

'Just make sure I get a look at them, and I'll forgive you for leaving those caricatures lying around.'

His face brightened. 'You've got it, Chelsea. Shall I make copies?'

'No, that's taking a risk. I only need to see them.'

A tap sounded at the door and Nick came in without waiting for permission.

'Here you go, Jim,' Chelsea said, and pushed a stack of meaningless drawings across the board to him with a look that spoke volumes. 'Thanks for waiting.'

He left in a hurry. Nick stood behind her for a few minutes, sipping his coffee and looking over her shoulder as she translated rough sketches into schematics that the clients would see. Finally Chelsea couldn't stand it any more. She tossed her pencil down and turned to him. 'If you want to do this house, help yourself. Or else get out of here and let me do it.'

He shook his head sadly. 'Don't you welcome the chance to teach me?'

'There isn't anything you want to learn from me.'

'Perhaps not in the office,' he said smoothly, and laughed as Chelsea's face flooded with colour. Then he bent over the drawing board. 'Where is the Sullivan house? I thought you'd be hard at work on it.'

'I'm certainly not going to let you see it till I'm finished.'

'Are you so uncertain of yourself?'

'Not at all. I just don't want you to steal my ideas.' She thought about those first sketches, of a three-level house snuggled into the side of the hill, and felt a quiet glow of pride. It was a good house. No matter what Nick did, he'd have trouble beating that design.

He made no comment. 'Let's get to work on the Jonas Building today.'

Chelsea's mouth dropped open. 'Not I,' she said with feeling.

'Why not?'

'I told you three days ago that I wasn't interested in that contest. Besides, I'm over my head with work now. I must have at least a dozen projects on the board, four under construction, and two that I haven't even thought about.'

'Then let's get busy and clean all these things up.' He loosened his tie and unbuttoned the collar of his silk shirt.

'I wish it was that easy.'

He speculated, 'You must be intrigued by the condos. Have you looked at the specs? There is plenty of space for about fifty units.'

'If it was just the condos, I might be interested,' Chelsea admitted.

'I went over to look at the building yesterday. With those lovely high ceilings it's a natural for conversion. And that centre bay you were telling me about would be ideal for indoor balconies.'

She shook her head. 'It sounds as if you've fallen in love with the building, after all.'

'Not necessarily. I still don't think it's a particularly valuable piece of architecture, but it's sturdy, and I still want to win that contest.' He stretched out on the couch and propped his feet up on the arm.

'Why are you lying on my couch?'

Nick shrugged. 'I offered to go to work, but it seems that you'd rather argue. I thought I might as well be comfortable while we discussed it.'

'I suppose you're hoping that Burke will walk in.'

He looked intrigued. 'It had never crossed my mind. Does he?'

'Never without knocking,' Chelsea snapped.

'Pity,' Nick murmured.

'And as for the Jonas Building,' she said, feeling the conversation slipping from her grasp, 'you needn't fear any competition from me. It sounds as if you have plenty of ideas already, and I'm certainly not going to fight you for the honours.'

'I'm not afraid of your competition. But it won't be easy for me. After all, I am the new kid in town.'

'And everybody still thinks you're wonderful. You shouldn't have any trouble getting the project all to yourself. No one on this staff is foolish enough to tangle with you.'

'Except you, Chelsea,' he said softly.

A flood of colour swept over her face. She said stubbornly, 'All you have to do is announce that you're going after it.'

'Maybe I don't want it by myself. I don't know enough yet about how this firm works.'

She looked up in mock amazement, her big eyes innocent. 'My God, there is something that Nicholas Stanton doesn't know?'

'Once in a while,' he said dryly. 'How about it? Do you want to do the condos?'

'Work with you on the Jonas Building?'

He nodded. 'Equal partners.'

Chelsea stared at him for a long time, eyes narrowed. Just what was he up to now, she wondered. 'Sorry, I'm too busy.'

'Would you rather I made it an order?'

'Why do you want me?'

'Because you know things about the city and the

firm that I don't. And you've done far more renovation work than I have.'

'So you're going to pick my brain.' She sipped her coffee thoughtfully and set the crystal mug safely on the corner of the desk. 'More likely you just want someone to share the blame if another firm brings in the winning design.'

'You'll get equal credit if we win.'

Chelsea was no fool. She knew what her name on a winning contest design could mean for her career, even if she was listed only as an assistant to Nicholas Stanton.

He let her think about it for a moment. Then he pulled up a stool. 'Where do I start? Construction specs? Do you have some blank forms?'

'That's the most boring part of a house. You're really serious, aren't you?'

'Never more so. You're going to help with this renovation, whether you want to or not. So you might as well work up some enthusiasm for the project.'

'How open-minded of you.' She thoughtfully tapped her triangle against the edge of the drawing board.

'Let's put it this way. If you decide not to work on the project, I have a lovely Christmas gift for Carl Shelby to hang in his office. And he won't have to wait till Christmas to get it.'

'What if I work with you? Will you give me those drawings back?' she asked shrewdly.

For a moment she thought he hadn't heard. Then he said, quietly, 'Sure. I'll give them back. In return for some real co-operation, of course.'

'I'll think about it,' she said. She pulled a set of drawings out of the cabinet and thrust them into his hands. 'Since you volunteered to help, you can start with these electrical plans while I'm thinking.'

'What's there to think about? Have I left you a

choice?' But he didn't push for an answer. He cleared
a space on her desk and started to work.

Chelsea sat there for a few minutes, her pencil idle,
staring out over the city. Her head was spinning. It
was an invitation she had never expected. All his
reasons sounded valid, and yet she didn't trust him an
inch. Nick Stanton shouldn't need anyone's help on a
project like the Jonas Building. So why was he asking
for hers?

She sighed, put a needle-sharp point on her pencil,
and started to work.

Marie came in a couple of hours later, and Chelsea
straightened her spine, sighed at the stiffness in her
muscles, and flexed her fingers. Two hours of
uninterrupted concentration had done wonders for
the work remaining to be done. She glanced over at
Nick, still sitting at her desk, and felt a spark of
amazement. He'd been so quiet that she'd forgotten
he was even there.

'Mr Shelby wants to see you, Miss Ryan,' Marie
said softly. 'He has a client with him.'

'If you don't mind, Nick?' Chelsea said, with more
than a hint of irony in her voice.

He looked up and smiled. 'I don't mind a bit. It
won't bother my work if you see a client here.'

'That wasn't quite what I meant. Would you please
leave?'

He leaned back in her desk chair and studied her,
not missing a detail. 'No, thanks,' he said pleasantly
and turned to a new drawing.

Marie was back by then, ushering in Carl Shelby
and an enormous bear of a man who made the senior
partner look something like a tugboat guiding an ocean
liner.

Chelsea gave up on dislodging Nick. 'Mr Bradley!'
she said, with genuine delight. 'I'm glad to see you
again.'

George Bradley stretched out a big hand and engulfed hers. 'Well, if it isn't little Chelsea Ryan,' he boomed. 'Your daddy told me you were prettier than ever, but I figured he was just opinionated.'

Chelsea couldn't help herself; she darted a look at Nick. He raised an eyebrow as if to say, Another victim, Chelsea?

'And this is Nick Stanton, our newest partner,' Shelby twittered, and George Bradley turned that wide grin on Nick. 'So you're the young man who's been changing the looks of public buildings all over Missouri,' he said.

'I have been doing my fair share of them,' Nick admitted.

Marie handed George a cup of coffee. He settled himself comfortably on the small couch beside Chelsea, his large hand making the plastic cup look like a toy, and said, 'That's why I'm here, young man. I like the looks of your buildings. Well, most of them, that is. Once in a while you go a bit too far. At any rate, I want one of those buildings for Norah Springs. The old home town, you understand how it is. I want the best.'

Chelsea could have screamed. If George Bradley wanted to build anything in Norah Springs, why hadn't he come to her first? To turn her town over to Nick Stanton . . .!

Nick cut neatly across the stream of chatter. 'Just what sort of building are you wanting, Mr Bradley?'

'Civic centre. Auditorium, place for the theatre club to have its shows. I'm sure you know the sort of thing.'

'Yes, indeed, Mr Bradley.' Nick's voice was smooth.

George Bradley looked fondly down at Chelsea and patted her shoulder. 'And I want this lady in on it, too. Chelsea knows just how much Norah Springs will stand for. She'll keep you in line, young man. Good taste, that's what we're after.'

Chelsea nearly laughed at the look on Nick's face, at the idea that any of his buildings could be considered not in good taste. But it was absolutely true, she told herself. Norah Springs wasn't quite ready for the kind of thing Nick had built in St Louis and Jefferson City.

Nick quickly recovered his poise. 'I'm sure we can design a civic centre that Norah Springs can be proud of, Mr Bradley.'

'That's great. Our board meets ten days from now— over Memorial Day weekend, as a matter of fact. Any chance you two could come up then? Look over the site, talk to the board, that kind of thing?'

My mother had something to do with this, Chelsea thought. Who else would arrange a meeting like that on a holiday weekend but a mother who wanted to have her daughter home for a few days?

'What about you, Chelsea?' Nick questioned. 'I have plans, but I can change them.'

'Of course. I can go that weekend.'

'Good!' George Bradley boomed. 'I'll make sure there's a reservation for you at the hotel, Mr Stanton. Of course Chelsea won't need to worry about a place to stay.' He grinned and patted her shoulder again. 'This little lady built my house a couple of years ago, you know. Did a fine job, too. A right fine job.' He hoisted himself to his feet. 'Look out for her, Mr Stanton. She has a way of getting what she wants.'

He was still booming when he and Shelby reached the lobby. Chelsea closed the office door behind them.

'Where the hell is Norah Springs?' Nick asked.

'About a hundred miles north of here. It's small, but definitely not the boondocks.'

'And he knows your father? Wonderful connections you have, don't you, Chelsea?'

'A few here and there,' she said, and wondered

which shade of red his face would turn the first time he was introduced to her father. It was an entertaining speculation.

'And you'll be staying at Mr Bradley's new house, that he's so proud of.'

Chelsea allowed herself a smile. 'Are you jealous that he doesn't have a room for you?'

'Not at all. I prefer my privacy. Especially when the alternative is watching—shall we say, inappropriate behaviour?'

Chelsea coloured, and said angrily, 'For your information, George Bradley has been married for fifty years and has a half-dozen grandchildren.'

'Well, Burke doesn't have the grandchildren, but otherwise . . .'

'I am tired of you saying nasty things about Burke!' Chelsea's temper flared, and she was beyond the point of wanting to control it. 'He adores Helen, and so does everyone else who knows her. No one wants to hurt that woman!'

'Want to or not, you seem to be doing a good job of it,' he said soberly. He picked up the documents he had been working on and left the room.

Chelsea slammed her fist down on the drawing board and the pencils jumped. 'And good riddance to you, Mr Stanton,' she snapped.

It was very late when she raised her head from the drawing board, and her spine was cramped from sitting so long in that unnatural position. Dusk had come while she worked. A couple of blocks to the south, the harsh lights of Busch Stadium glowed, and inside the round arena she could see the seething crowd watching a baseball game. 'It's nice that someone has time for recreation,' she thought. Yes, a weekend at home, even if it involved some work, would be good for her.

She sighed and turned back to the drawings.

There was a tap at her door, and Nick looked in.

'What do you want?' Chelsea asked wearily.

'Something to eat.'

'I don't hide a smorgasbord in my desk drawer. Eileen keeps sugar cookies in her file cabinet, and Carl has a fully-stocked bar, but . . .'

'I was thinking in terms of a complete meal, at a restaurant.'

'Try Angelo's downstairs. I can recommend the manicotti.' She turned back to her drawing.

He hesitated a split second. 'Want to keep me company?'

'Must I?'

'No, but you've been here twelve hours today. And you didn't have lunch.' He pulled the knot of his tie and settled his shirt collar.

'You're wrong about that. Marie brought me a sandwich.'

'After working that long without a break, you can't be doing anything constructive for your clients.'

'I should have known it was the clients you were worried about.'

'Isn't that the whole point? Come on, Chelsea, stop arguing. You know you're hungry.'

She looked at the drawing, which swam before her eyes, and then the spicy aroma of manicotti seemed to float through the office, tickling her nose. 'All right.'

It was late enough that the crowd at Angelo's was beginning to thin, but the restaurant was never quiet. The *maitre d'* led them to a table tucked away in a corner, and Nick sat down with a sigh. 'They specialise in privacy, don't they?'

'Yes. All the executives bring their secretaries here for intimate little lunches.' Then she flushed red. If he says anything more about Burke, she thought . . .

Nick didn't seem to hear. 'I'd forgotten how much work it is to do the specs for a house,' he said, and rubbed his eyes.

'Nobody likes houses. I don't understand, Nick. I know they're hard work and the fee isn't nearly as large as in the bigger projects, but there is so much joy in creating space for a family, on a budget they can afford. And then watching the house go up, and the family move in ...' She shook her head. 'I can't describe the feeling.'

'Wouldn't you get the same thrill from the condos in the Jonas Building?'

'No. There is no individuality in condos—all the units are alike.'

'If they turn out that way in the Jonas Building,' he said, 'you will have only yourself to blame.'

She stared at him for a full minute. 'I hadn't considered that possibility.'

'See? That's why I'm the partner and you're the lowly staffer.'

Chelsea shook her head. 'I doubt that it would be practical.'

'I'm really amazed that you aren't excited by that building. You seem fascinated by other old places.'

'Old houses,' Chelsea corrected firmly. 'I love to renovate and remodel them.'

'Like Hillhaven.'

She couldn't find a trace of sarcasm in his voice then, and so she nodded slowly. 'It's a pretty house. There are hundreds of them out there, structurally sound but deteriorated. Have you been down to Laclede's Landing, right by the riverfront?'

'Not yet.'

'If you'd been looking when you went to the riverboat the other night, you could have seen part of it. That whole nine-block area is coming back to life, after years of standing empty and desolate and falling down. I'd like to do for the houses of St Louis what has been done for the Landing. There are so many old treasures.'

'Which do you like better—old houses or new?'

Chelsea considered, and the waiter put a steaming plate in front of her. She breathed deeply of the sharp tomato scent and said, 'That's hard. The challenge of renovation, against the sheer freedom of starting out with an empty lot—I don't know. What about you?'

'It isn't houses at all for me, you know. So I don't care much which kind, as long as I don't get stuck with too many of them.'

Chelsea shook her head. 'I couldn't disagree with you more. I like the variety in single-family houses. Besides, I don't think I could stay interested in one project for months or years at a stretch. I like change.'

There was a brief silence, as if Nick was debating with himself about whether to answer. Then he said, 'Have you ever designed a place for yourself?'

'Half a dozen times.'

'Have you built it yet?'

'No. I'm still living in a little cardboard box out on the west edge of town.'

He laughed at that. 'And the shoemaker's kids go barefoot, too.'

'That's right. Why invest in a house? I may not live here for long.'

'Why not? You could always sell it.'

'I'm not sure the house I want would be saleable. I want to burrow underground, you see. Not many people get turned on by that.'

'I never would have suspected you of being a hermit. Building a cave and crawling away to hide in it—for shame, Chelsea.'

'I'm not a hermit,' she denied. 'The house I want will be built around an atrium covered by a glass bubble. Even underground, it will have more light than the average house, and it will be quieter and more private.'

'I can hear you now, on the 'phone to the police. "Officer, someone is bubble-peeking!" ' Nick mocked gently.

Chelsea stood her ground. 'With the earth berm and a flagstone floor in the atrium, it will just about heat itself with passive solar. And . . .'

'You're going to have trouble getting it past the zoning board.'

'I know.' She cut another slice of bread off the crusty loaf. 'That's probably the biggest reason for not building it now. Why must zoning laws be twenty years behind technology?'

Nick shrugged. 'Because now and then they're right and technology is wrong, I suppose. It makes it unnecessarily hard on us. Are you serious about not staying in St Louis?'

She was instantly suspicious. 'Why do you want to know?'

Nick shrugged. 'You're the one who brought up the subject, Chelsea.'

'I'll probably be at Shelby Harris till I'm old and grey,' she said.

'Unless something happens to prevent it,' he agreed.

Chelsea moved the last bit of manicotti around on her plate and thought about throwing it at him. Calm down, she told herself. He's right; you're the one who said you might not stay. Be smart, and change the subject. 'I might look into building a dome home,' she said finally.

'What kind? Geodesic? Plastic? Concrete?'

'Foam, I think. The kind they're building out on the West Coast. There's a seminar offered next autumn in Los Angeles, and I'd like to go and find out how they'd work around here.'

'Sounds good. Let me see the details, and we'll try to work it out.'

Chelsea sighed. She'd forgotten that he'd have to approve any travelling she did from now on. 'Yes, Boss,' she said, keeping her tone as even as possible.

Nick's eyebrows went up, but he didn't comment. 'Want something for dessert?'

'No, I'm ready to go back to work.'

He signalled the waiter for the bill. 'How about some fresh air first?'

'If you call it fresh.' Chelsea reached for her purse. 'What's my share of that?'

'Your share is precisely nothing. I invited you.'

'Nick, I wouldn't have come if I hadn't intended to pay for my own meal.'

'Do you think I don't know that?' Nick pushed his chair back. 'If it makes you feel better, the next one is on you.'

'I don't like owing you anything,' Chelsea told him frankly.

It was the first time she had heard him really laugh. He tucked her hand into his arm as soon as they reached the street. 'Tell me about Norah Springs and George Bradley. Sounds as if they're having an affair, doesn't it?'

'Just as long as you don't think I'm sleeping with him,' Chelsea muttered. 'George is the premiere citizen of the Springs. Small-town boy made good in the city, that sort of thing. Just don't be fooled by that country-boy talk of his, because he's no fool. A couple of years ago he retired, sold his manufacturing business here in St Louis, and went back to the old home town.'

'And built a big new house . . .' he prompted.

'Ballroom, music room—the whole caboodle, George's wife likes to think she's musical, so there is always a string quartet playing when she throws a dinner party. She's trying to bring culture to the Springs.'

'So it's really her idea?'

'Oh, I don't think so. Norah Springs was quietly cultured long before Elsie Bradley took it over. By the way, be sure to take a dinner jacket.'

'You're joking.'

'No. It's required at Elsie Bradley's table. Which

reminds me, I'll have to get something. She's seen every dress I own.'

'Does Norah Springs need a civic centre?'

Chelsea nodded. 'Oh, yes. And the acoustics had better be as good as anything in St Louis, or you'll have trouble.'

Nick looked down at her quizzically. 'Don't you mean, we'll have trouble?'

'This one is strictly your department, Nick,' she said. 'Remember? I'm only going along to keep you straight on what fits into Norah Springs.'

'What makes you the expert? Building Bradley's house?'

'And a few other things. I grew up in Norah Springs.'

'I see method in the madness. What happens if I go beserk and design something totally inappropriate?'

Chelsea smiled sweetly. 'If you are nice to me in the meantime, I'll rescue you from the tar and feathers. Otherwise . . .'

Nick tightened his grip on her hand and started across the street.

'Don't you think we'd better go back? The only thing down this way is the parking ramp.'

'I know. I'm sending you home.' He turned in at the entrance.

'I wanted to work a while.'

'So come in early tomorrow. In the meantime, go home and read a good book. That's an order.'

He spotted the Mercedes right away in the almost empty floor, and he put her firmly into the driver's seat. She rolled down the window to protest, and he leaned on the door, arms folded. 'My car's up a level if you'd like me to follow you home—make sure you get there safely.'

'I'm a grown woman, Nick. I can drive myself across town.'

'After riding with you, I'm not so sure,' he muttered.

For a moment, there in the dim light, she thought she saw something flare in his eyes. Was he going to kiss her? she thought a little breathlessly.

But he just said, 'I'll see you tomorrow,' and stepped back from the car. He was still standing there when the Mercedes coasted down the ramp and out to the street.

CHAPTER SIX

'DON'T sweat it,' Jim said, his voice low but stern. 'You have that bet won hands down.'

Chelsea shook her head. 'Something is wrong. I can feel it.' She leaned against the corridor wall, a Shelby Harris portfolio containing her drawings of the Sullivan house in her hand. She was waiting for Nick, and she was getting uncomfortably warm in the belted raincoat.

'Oh, don't go getting female intuition on me,' Jim begged. 'I can't take it. You saw Nick's design. It was . . .'

'It's competent,' Chelsea interrupted.

Jim nodded. 'That's about the best word for it. And yours is original, it fits the site . . .'

Chelsea wasn't listening. 'I didn't expect Nick to design something that is merely competent.'

'Come on, Chelsea. He's a whizz at office buildings and factories, but he doesn't do houses. He's competing out of his own territory. Besides, you know you have it won. Don't be such a worrier.'

Chelsea smiled reluctantly. Her design was better; she knew that it was not prejudice. 'I just won't be comfortable till he admits that I've beaten him,' she admitted.

'Well, the professor will do that for you soon enough,' Jim consoled. He waved a casual hand and vanished down the hall. He was doing that a lot since Nick Stanton had joined the firm, Chelsea thought; he seemed to possess some sort of radar that warned him whenever Nick was coming around a corner.

And Jim was right again, Chelsea realised as Nick's office door opened. He was elegantly tailored today in

88

light grey, a dark blue shirt setting off the even tan of his skin. The portfolio he carried was identical to the one in Chelsea's hand, and she looked at it with a sudden flash of confidence. Nick had made a mistake when he took her on in her own speciality, and he was going to pay for that mistake.

He set the portfolio down and pulled a trenchcoat on. 'Of all the days it has to choose to rain,' he said with a note of disgust in his voice. 'Are you ready? The professor will be waiting for us.'

'I'm not only ready, I'm eager to hear what he has to say,' Chelsea said and started down the hall. 'I hope you aren't too disappointed at the results.'

Nick's eyebrows arched. 'A little over-confident, aren't you?' he asked softly, falling into step beside her.

'I have reason to be,' Chelsea murmured.

He didn't seem to hear. 'Besides, I happen to think you're the one who will be disappointed.'

'Now who's sounding overconfident?' she warned. 'Let's take the Mercedes.'

'Only if you promise not to drive,' Nick countered.

'It's my car,' she snapped as they entered the parking garage.

'And it's one of the miracles of the modern world that it's still in one piece.' He reached for the keys, and after a moment's hesitation, Chelsea handed them over. Let him have his moment of glory, she thought. Her victory would soon knock him out of the water.

He whistled as they drove through the light summer rain, keeping rhythm with the windshield wipers. He sounded cheerful and not at all concerned about the outcome of this bet. Then he broke off abruptly to say, 'Nice car. I'm sure you enjoy the distinction of being one of the privileged few.'

'I like it,' Chelsea said, just a little warily.

'It's a pretty toy. But aren't you afraid to get it wet?'

'A car is a car, Nick. How would I keep it dry, for heaven's sake?'

He didn't answer. 'Who gave it to you? Burke, or was it the gentleman from the riverboat?'

'Perhaps it was neither of them.'

It didn't seem to bother him. 'In fact, possibly you don't even remember.' He wheeled the car into the driveway beside the professor's house and turned to her with a smile. 'What do you say, Chelsea? Shall we save the professor some time—do you want to concede now and get it over with?'

Chelsea saw red. 'I certainly do not,' she snapped. 'If you think you can bluff me, Nick Stanton, you're crazy!'

He shrugged. 'Come along, then.'

The professor was one of the grand old men of architecture in the city. They had spent a whole afternoon in Chelsea's office arguing before finally settling on him as the arbiter of the contest. No one in the firm would do, especially not Carl Shelby or Frank Harris, Chelsea had said. Neither of them would see any humour in the competition, to begin with, she argued, and besides, Nick would have an unfair advantage. She'd just as soon the partners didn't even know about this little spree, until after she'd won it, Chelsea thought. Then she'd make sure there was a splash!

Nick had solemnly agreed to her demands, but then added that he would not trust any male under the age of seventy because then Chelsea would have an advantage. It was the closest she had ever come to throwing something at him.

The professor was waiting for them at the door. He was stooped with age now, but his eyes were still bright, and he smiled under the droopy moustache that was his trademark. 'So we have a contest,' he said as he hung up their wet coats. 'Come in, come in. There isn't enough excitement in buildings these days? You need to make your own contests?'

'This is a little different than most,' Nick said. 'This is to settle a bet.'

The professor's eyes gleamed. 'I see,' he said in his soft voice, and Chelsea wondered just what he thought was going on. It made her a little uneasy, as if the professor thought he was dealing with a couple of lovers!

'Let's see the plans,' he said. 'You go set them up in the next room. Just prop them up anywhere, and let me know when you're ready. Shall I get you something to drink, Miss Ryan? How about a beer, Nick?'

Nick shook his head. 'Not during working hours. Thanks anyway, Professor.'

The old man looked disappointed. 'Then I'll bring some iced tea.'

'That would be fine,' Nick said. 'Give us five minutes to set these things up, Professor.'

Chelsea said, her teeth gritted, 'You didn't tell me you were on a first-name basis with him.'

Nick shrugged and tried to look innocent.

Chelsea glared at him and went on into the living room. She was setting up her display when Nick brought his portfolio in, and she concentrated very hard on getting her drawings at just the right angle. The front elevation was the most important, the view as the house would appear from the street. She fussed with it, getting it to stand up just right.

Nick opened his portfolio, took out a series of mounted drawings, and lined them up on the couch. He was very casual about the whole thing. Then he sat down across the room and observed Chelsea.

'If you're so confident, why are you nervous?' he asked finally.

She tossed her head, making the auburn waves bounce on her shoulders, and came to sit down. 'I happen to think the presentation of the plans is sometimes just as important as the plans themselves.'

'Not with the professor. He isn't going to be fooled by any tricks like that.'

'Tricks!' Chelsea sputtered. 'If you're going to talk

about tricks——' She turned her back on him indignantly, and her eyes fell for the first time on his design. 'Oh, my God . . .' she breathed.

The house seemed to hang from the side of the ravine, as airy as a spider's web. The steel of its framework gave it strength, yet the glass walls left it looking as delicate as a fairy castle.

'Do you like it?' Nick asked politely.

She turned on him with the fury of a wounded tiger. 'That's not the house Jim . . .' she stumbled and stopped.

'Cheated, did you?' he asked. 'I thought you would.'

'I did not cheat!' Chelsea wailed. 'I designed my house just as I would have if it hadn't been a bet. I only wanted . . .'

'You only wanted an advance peek at the competition. And I simply made sure you got it. It just didn't happen to be my final design, that's all.'

'This is nothing like the first one,' Chelsea said, with all the dignity she could muster.

Nick grinned. 'So who says only a woman can change her mind?'

The professor came in with a tray. He handed out the glasses and looked speculatively at Chelsea, who had put one hand on her throbbing head.

'It looks as if we won't even have to bother you, Professor,' Nick said smoothly. 'The lady has conceded.'

Chelsea sat up. 'The lady has conceded nothing,' she said, her voice a little shrill. 'I was surprised, that's all.'

The professor tried to hide a smile. Then he walked over to the couch and looked at the two sets of drawings. He studied them both, then he tapped Nick's. 'This one surprised you, little one?' he asked, his eyes intent on Chelsea.

She nodded reluctantly.

'It's a surprising house,' the professor continued. He sipped his iced tea and continued to look from one to the other. 'Using the techniques of a skyscraper to build a residence—it's very interesting, Nick.'

'Thank you, Professor,' Nick said modestly. Chelsea could have cheerfully dumped her iced tea over his head.

'Now, from what you have told me about the clients, and from what I know of the neighbourhood ...' There was a long pause. 'For sheer beauty and grace, this one.' He thumped a finger loudly against Nick's drawing.

Nick relaxed and turned a self-satisfied smile to her. 'Are you ready to concede now, Chelsea?' he asked softly.

'Don't hurry me, young man,' the professor snapped. 'For the practical needs of the client, this one.' He waved the front elevation of Chelsea's house under Nick's nose.

Chelsea would have given a great deal at that moment to have had a camera. The look of utter disbelief that spread across Nick's face should have been preserved for future ages, she thought; it was so very well done.

'And the winner?' Nick asked. His voice was a little hoarse.

The professor smiled, an expression of singular sweetness. 'I declare it a draw,' he said softly. 'I suggest you learn to work together, instead of competing, and let the vision and the practicality go hand in hand. Then you will go far.'

It had something of the note of a benediction about it. There was nothing else left to say, and they packed up the drawings in silence.

Chelsea drove back to the office. There was not a word spoken all the way.

Jim saw her come in and met her at the door of her office. 'Well?' he asked eagerly.

Chelsea silenced him with a finger to her lips. Once inside the room, she hung up her wet coat and flung herself down on the couch. 'I didn't win,' she said.

Jim looked stunned. 'The professor has lost his touch,' he declared.

Chelsea shook her head and told him what had happened. 'The house you drew for Nick wasn't the real one. He gave it to you because he knew you'd show it to me, and he drew the real one himself. I don't know why I didn't expect that.'

'It makes sense,' Jim admitted. 'That guy is the most suspicious character I've ever met.'

'Are you just figuring that out?' Chelsea asked tartly. She stood up. 'Well, I'd better get the plans ready to show the Sullivans this evening.' She opened the portfolio.

'It's beautiful,' Jim breathed as he caught sight of the top drawing.

'If you think this is nice you should see Nick's,' Chelsea told him. Then she looked down at the drawings she held, and stopped dead. 'He took the wrong portfolio out of the car,' she said. 'We both had Shelby Harris portfolios—and he was in such a hurry he grabbed the wrong one.'

'What are you going to do, Chelsea?' Jim asked with avid interest. 'Tear them up?'

'Destroy anything this beautiful?' She was concentrating on Nick's drawings as she spoke, and in the back of her mind the professor's words rang out. They could have both beauty and practicality, he had said . . .

'Out, Jim,' she ordered, and shut the door tight behind him.

The next morning, bright and early, she tapped on Nick's office door, the crystal mug of coffee in her hand. He sounded grumpy, she thought, when he called, 'Come in, if you must.'

'Good morning,' Chelsea announced from the threshhold.

Nick's eyebrows drew together. 'Oh, it's you.'

'I thought you'd be delighted to see me. After yesterday, you know, I don't have to consult you about anything I'm working on.'

'That's not quite what happened.'

'Well, let's not argue about details, shall we? I just came to tell you that the Sullivans were very intrigued by the preliminary house plans. They took them home to show her brother, the contractor. I hate to work with that man,' she added thoughtfully. 'Rumour has it that he once read a book on how to build a house, and now he thinks he's an authority.'

'Will you stop babbling?'

'Must you be irritable? I thought you'd like to know that it went well.'

Nick sat down in the big leather chair behind his desk. 'You're only here so you can enjoy my defeat.'

'Actually, I thought you'd like to see the plans.'

'I looked them over thoroughly yesterday, thank you.'

'That was yesterday,' Chelsea said gently. 'It took hours of hard work to make my practical and efficient interior fit into your beautiful and graceful exterior, but . . .'

Nick rocked his chair back, and put his feet up on the corner of his desk. His eyebrows were still fierce. 'You redesigned it? Combined the drawings?'

'The best features of both,' Chelsea said modestly.

He grunted. 'That's a matter of judgment, and I don't always trust yours.'

'I realise that. When it comes time to do the actual blueprints we will probably fight over every line. But as the professor said, your drawings didn't really address the needs of the client.'

'I'll argue that, too. How long has it been since the professor designed a house?'

'Come on, Nick. You and I together couldn't catch up with him by the time we're sixty.' Chelsea walked over to the wide windows that faced out over the river.

How was it possible, she wondered vaguely, that Nick's office, just down the hall from hers, had a much better view?

He had moved so silently that she had not heard him, and she was startled when he spoke, for he was standing right behind her. 'You and I together,' he quoted gravely. 'How about it, Chelsea?'

She stood there frozen for a moment, wondering why her pulse was fluttering so.

'Shall we be partners on the Jonas Building, too?' There was a brief pause. 'Wrangling over every decision will make us both better architects, you know.'

Professional partners. Chelsea's heart rate slowed a little. She turned around, and had to look a long way up to meet his eyes.

He was holding out his hand, and she put hers into it. 'Partners,' she said, a little breathlessly.

His hand was warm. Chelsea let her fingers slip out of his grasp. 'I'd better get back to work,' she said.

He didn't try to prevent her from leaving. 'Let's start on the Jonas Building this afternoon,' he said. He sat down at his desk and pulled a stack of papers across the blotter.

All they had agreed to was to work together, Chelsea scolded herself as she walked back to her own office. So why should she feel that she had made some sort of vow?

'I've already explained why I want to take the Mercedes to Norah Springs,' Chelsea argued. 'It's already packed, for one thing——'

'So is my car,' Nick interrupted.

'And I want to get the engine tuned while I'm home.'

His eyebrows went sky-high. 'On a holiday weekend?'

'Obviously, you don't know Norah Springs.'

'I can't wait to learn,' Nick said sourly.

'So I'll follow you over to your apartment, and we'll transfer your luggage into the Mercedes and . . .'

'Does it have air bags?'

'No. Why?'

'If you're driving, I want all the protection I can get.'

Chelsea put her hands on her hips. 'I'll have you know, Nick Stanton, that in more than ten years of driving I have never so much as scratched a fender!' She realised abruptly that he was paying more attention to the way her beige trouser suit clung to her curves than to what she was saying. 'It's three o'clock, Nick. If we're going to be in Norah Springs by the time the holiday traffic picks up, we'd better leave soon.'

He grinned. 'You're so cute when you're mad. All right, you win.'

Chelsea was speechless. Nick picked up his briefcase and stopped at the door. 'Are you coming?' he asked. 'Or have you decided to turn into a statue?'

He didn't wait for an answer. Instead, he paused beside his secretary's desk. 'Miss Ryan and I are off for the weekend,' he said.

Chelsea recovered her voice by the time he had tossed his briefcase into the Mercedes. 'You didn't need to make it sound like a rendezvous!' she snapped.

'Did I?'

'You know quite well you did. You probably planned it that way.'

He had the grace to look ashamed of himself, then abruptly he grinned. 'If the typing pool is going to start rumours anyway, we might as well enjoy ourselves this weekend,' he suggested.

'I'm not dumb enough to have an affair with you,' Chelsea snapped.

Nick looked hurt. 'It sounded like a lot of fun to me.'

'I'm sure it did. And it would probably be even more fun when you could fire me next week.'

'Why would I want to do that? You're actually quite good at what you do.'

'I suppose it should be some comfort that you've finally noticed!' She put the car into gear.

She followed him to his apartment and waited patiently as he transferred a leather suitcase to the Mercedes. By the time everything was arranged, and he settled himself in the passenger seat, Chelsea had cooled off somewhat.

Nick fastened his seatbelt, tested it with a jerk, and leaned back with a sigh. 'Well, I've done all I can do to protect myself. The rest is up to my guardian angel.'

The Mercedes' tyres squealed on the pavement.

Nick winced and added, 'I don't quite understand, you know.'

'Understand what?'

'Why you turned me down. Frankly, Chelsea, Burke is getting old professionally. His name doesn't carry the same weight that it used to in the field. I think you'd be wise to look around for a new patron.'

'I have never needed a patron, as you so politely put it. I think of Burke as—as an uncle. Nothing more.'

'Strange family you have,' Nick commented. 'By the way, that truck is a little larger than the car, I'd appreciate it if you wouldn't challenge him for his half of the highway.'

Chelsea bit her tongue. The look she gave him should have shrivelled him up to a crisp.

Nick didn't seem to notice. 'Are we taking the River Road?'

'It's the most scenic.'

'Also the most curvy, narrow and dangerous,' he pointed out.

'If you're so afraid of travelling——'

'I'm not. It's just your driving that panics me.'

Chelsea slammed on the brakes and pulled the car to a stop on the verge of the road. 'So why don't you drive, instead?' she said coldly. 'That way I can enjoy my favourite route up to Norah Springs in peace!'

'Sounds good to me.' He unfastened his safety belt and walked around the car. Chelsea settled herself with a flounce in the passenger seat and stared out the window, determined to pay no attention to him for the two-hour drive.

The effort was doomed to failure. Nick talked gently on subject after subject, sometimes answering himself where called for, until Chelsea gave in.

'Does it bother you to spend three days in Norah Springs?' she asked finally. 'You said you had plans for the weekend.'

Nick shrugged. 'It was nothing important. There will be other weekends.'

Chelsea thought about that for a moment. 'She must be very understanding,' she said finally.

Nick grinned. 'What makes you think it was a woman?' he asked innocently, but there was a smile in his voice.

There had to be a woman, she mused. They probably threw themselves in piles at Nick's feet. Just because Chelsea didn't find him appealing didn't mean that other women weren't intrigued by that boyish charm.

There must be a woman, and yet the office grapevine didn't seem to know anything about his private life.

Chelsea was startled when she sighted the big sign announcing Norah Springs. 'We can't be here yet,' she announced, and checked her watch to find that two hours had indeed passed.

'I wondered if you were ever coming back out of your episode of deep thought.'

She ignored him. 'Take a left at the first intersection,' she instructed.

'Is that the way to the hotel?'

'No. It's downtown. But you'll probably need the car tonight, so you can drop me off first.'

'Is George providing you with transportation?' Nick asked. He didn't sound interested.

'I shouldn't need any, Should I?' Chelsea retorted.

Nick shrugged. 'I suppose not, if all the events are at his house.' He made the turn on to a winding, quiet street. Most of the houses were set well back from the street on large, landscaped lots. 'Nice neighbourhood.'

'There's the house I grew up in.' Chelsea waved a careless hand.

Nick slowed the Mercedes to look at the blue and white split-level. 'Not what I would have expected,' he said.

'Unlike you, I wasn't born an architect,' she said coolly. 'Turn right up here.'

This street was newer, and wilder. The lots were more as nature had intended, and the houses were larger and farther apart. Most of them looked as if they had grown right there on the site. 'The one on your left is George Bradley's,' Chelsea pointed out.

The Mercedes slowed to a crawl as Nick studied the cedar-shingled exterior of the house. 'Where do I park?' he asked.

'At the house across the street. I'm staying with my parents.'

The car swerved a little as he turned to look at her. 'But you pointed out that split-level . . .'

'I said I grew up there, not that Mom and Dad still lived there. You assume an awful lot, don't you, Nick? No one ever said I was staying at the Bradley's either.'

It was the first time she'd ever seen him at a loss for words. He pulled the Mercedes up in the circular drive beside the Ryan's forest green house.

'Chelsea!' Sara came across the drive just as Chelsea opened her car door. 'Oh, darling, it's so good to have you home!'

'Believe me, it feels wonderful from this side too,' Chelsea murmured. 'Mom, this is Nick Stanton, my new boss. Sara Ryan, who has the singular honour of being my mother.'

'Nick, do come in for coffee.' Sara urged Chelsea towards the house. 'We can unload all the luggage later.'

'I'm only home for the weekend, Mom. I brought one tote bag—that's all.'

'More's the pity,' Sara murmured. 'Well, we'll just do the best we can. Let's have coffee on the gallery.'

'The gallery?' Nick asked.

'Yes. It's my favourite room. I couldn't express it very well when I tried to tell Chelsea what I wanted, but she seemed to read my mind.' Sara led the way into the great family room that stretched the length of the house, looking out over the tangled growth on the hill. Today the long windows stood open and the May breeze teased the leaves of the green plants that formed the only curtains. Nick walked across the room and stood staring thoughtfully out across the hillside and the fenced-in swimming pool that lay below the house.

Sara poured coffee. 'Cream and sugar, Nick?'

He shook his head. 'Neither, thanks.' He waved a hand out to the view. 'It's nice, Chelsea.'

'Should I take that as a compliment?'

One eybrow arched. 'Take it however you like. It was meant to be one.'

'Chelsea, come get your cup,' her mother ordered. 'Nick, you must be an unusual person. I can think of only a couple of others who have been allowed to drive Chelsea's car.' She smiled.

Mother, don't do this to me, Chelsea pleaded silently. Please don't get started with stories about when your darling was little. I can't take it.

'Where's Dad?' Chelsea asked, hoping to get her mother's attention refocused.

'Oh, he'll be home soon,' Sara went on. 'A late appointment—they always happen when he most wants to get out of the office early. I hope you can join us for dinner, Nick. Josh is going to grill steaks.'

Nick's eyes met Chelsea's, and a gleam of humour sprang to life in those blue depths. 'I'd love to, Mrs Ryan.'

'If the Bradleys are expecting you, I can just give them a call. Of course, Elise has probably already spotted the car. She always knows everything that happens over here.'

Nick looked a bit puzzled. 'I'm staying at the hotel, Mrs Ryan, not with the Bradley's.'

Sara looked up, startled. 'Do you know, I'd forgotten that they built that enormous house with only one bedroom. Chelsea, I'm ashamed of you for letting them do it.'

'That makes two of us,' Nick murmured. 'Why only one bedroom?'

'I built exactly what they wanted. George told me,' Chelsea explained patiently, 'that he'd had all the overnight guests anyone should be expected to put up with in a lifetime, and he wasn't ever going to have another one. From now on, all his guests have to go home after dinner.'

Sara sniffed. 'So there they are, those two old people with their elaborate house, and not even a place to tuck a baby grandchild away for the night.'

Chelsea laughed. 'That doesn't upset George a bit. And an afternoon with his grandchildren would probably drive even you wild, Mom.'

'But to send your own children to a hotel!'

'He owns the hotel, Mom.'

'I don't care, Chelsea. It's still inhuman. And how they think they'll ever sell that huge house . . .' Sara shook her head.

'George doesn't intend to. He'll laugh from heaven—or wherever—while the kids try to get rid of it.'

Sara ignored the interruption. 'But speaking of the hotel, Nick, it makes no sense for you to be all the way downtown when you can stay right here with Chelsea.'

A wicked sparkle flared in Nick's eyes. 'With Chelsea?' he murmured.

Chelsea said, keeping her composure as well as she could, 'Mom always keeps the guest room ready.' And just wait till I get a chance to talk to her about this, Chelsea resolved.

'I'd be honoured,' Nick said.

'That's taken care of, then. Why don't you two bring in your luggage and get settled? There are just a few things I need to finish about dinner.' She paused in the doorway. 'Chelsea, there are some new things hanging in your closet. I thought a new dress might come in handy for the weekend.'

'Mother . . .' But Sara was gone. Chelsea shook her head.

Nick was unloading the car when she caught up with him.

'My mother likes to manage things,' Chelsea said, and picked up her briefcase.

'I can see that,' he said gravely.

'If she wasn't right all the time, it would be infuriating.'

A horn beeped and Chelsea looked up as a sporty bright red car turned into the driveway. She set the briefcase down and waved.

Josh Ryan unfolded himself from the driver's seat. 'Chelsea! How's my darlin' today?'

'Just fine, Daddy,' she said demurely, and looked up at Nick, whose face had gone white. The taste of revenge was sweet indeed, she told herself. The look on Nick's face almost made up for all the nasty things he'd said to her all week.

Almost, she added. She owed him a few surprises yet.

CHAPTER SEVEN

BUT nothing could keep Nick silent for long. By the time the steaks were cooking, he and Josh were on the best of terms out on the patio beside the pool, and Chelsea, drinking dry sherry on the gallery with her mother, could have screamed.

It just wasn't fair, she thought, half-listening as her mother chatted on. Then she realised that Sara had stopped talking, and looked up. 'What, Mother?'

'What is wrong with you, Chelsea? I don't believe you've heard a word I've said.'

'Sorry, Mom. I'm really tired these days. Overwork, I suppose.'

Sara's face reflected instant concern. 'You need a vacation, dear. Why don't you stay for a couple of weeks and rest?'

Chelsea shook her head. 'Perhaps later in the summer. But right now there is just too much work to do.'

'Well, at least don't work too hard this weekend. All you have to do, after all, is go to Bradley's cocktail party on Sunday and listen to all the plans for the civic centre.'

'Nick will want to look at the site, and . . .' Chelsea was suddenly so tired she could scarcely hold her head up.

'So let him,' Sara ordered. 'That doesn't mean you have to go with him.'

'Why did you invite him to stay, Mom?'

'I'm surprised at you, Chelsea. It was the only polite thing to do.' She looked at her daughter with a speculative gleam in her eyes. 'He seems to be a very nice man.'

'Most men set out to charm you, Mom. There's something about you that they want to impress.'

Sara patted her daughter's hand. 'It's sweet of you to say that. And it might even have been true twenty years ago, dear.'

'It doesn't mean that they're all really charming underneath, though. And Nick certainly isn't.'

'I still think he's delightful. The barbecue is tomorrow, by the way. It's out at the country club.'

'The civic centre thing? I thought you said it was Sunday.'

Sara looked at her with aggravation in her eyes. 'You really are tired, aren't you, Chelsea? The barbecue for your old classmates, I mean. You are going, aren't you?'

Chelsea groaned. 'I don't suppose I have a choice, do I?'

'I thought you'd like to see them.'

'There isn't much we have in common any more, Mom. Most of them are married with a couple of kids, and here I am——'

Sara softened. 'There's nothing wrong with being unmarried at your age, Chelsea. The right man will come along, you'll see. And as for children—well, there is plenty of time.'

'It isn't that, Mom. It's just that it isn't very comfortable being alone in a group of couples.'

'Well, you and Nick can go play golf tomorrow and then to the barbecue.'

Chelsea turned from the portable bar where she was refilling her sherry glass. 'Why would I want to take Nick along?'

'He is your guest, Chelsea.'

'No, Mom. He's YOUR guest. I didn't invite him to stay here.'

There was a momentary silence, and then Josh called from downstairs, 'Are you two coming down, or will Nick and I have to eat all this food by ourselves?'

'Don't you dare, Dad. I'm starving!' Chelsea called back. 'Mom, Nick is my boss. He is not my friend, or my boyfriend, or anything else, and he's never likely to be.'

'Did I say he should be?'

'Besides, I've known him three weeks longer than you have, and believe me, you don't know what he's really like. Trust me, all right?'

'Shall I hide the family silver?' Sara asked drily. She didn't wait for an answer, just picked up her glass and led the way down to the patio.

Nick held Sara's chair, and said, 'Josh tells me you did the portrait of Chelsea. The one in the gallery, with the daisies in her hand.'

Sara glanced up with a smile. 'Oh, yes. I think she was four years old.'

'She couldn't have been much older than that,' Nick observed.

'If anyone says anything about my chubby cheeks, I will leave the table,' Chelsea announced.

'That was from my short-lived photographic career,' Sara continued. 'But I never could master the mechanics of a camera, so I had to go back to oils.'

'You're an artist, then?'

'Quite a combination, aren't we?' Josh volunteered as he put Chelsea's steak down in front of her. 'Chelsea's an artist, too, you know. Have you seen any of her sketches, Nick?'

Chelsea swallowed hard, but Nick merely grinned wickedly at her and said, 'I've had the pleasure, Josh.'

'Yes, she's her mother's child, of course. I like to think that the taste for maths and logic came from me, but at any rate, Chelsea couldn't have turned out as anything but an architect.'

'Dad, please,' Chelsea sighed. 'Can we talk about something else?'

'Don't be so modest,' Nick said innocently. 'You're a fascinating topic of conversation, Chelsea.'

'Dad, do you suppose the garage could fit the Mercedes in for a tune-up tomorrow?' she asked, desperate to change the subject. 'The engine has been running a bit rough.'

'I didn't notice anything wrong with it today,' Nick disagreed. 'In fact, I've never driven a car that handled so well.'

Chelsea looked down at her plate and waited. She knew what was coming next.

'Chelsea let you drive the Mercedes?' Josh asked. 'She's never even let me drive that car, and I'm the one who paid for it.'

Nick's eyes, glowing with laughter, met Chelsea's across the table. I hope he's happy now that he knows where the car came from, she thought. 'The only people who drive my car are the male chauvinist pigs who won't take no for an answer,' she said acidly.

Nick smiled. 'Congratulations, Chelsea. You have finally discovered the essence of my character. I am never discouraged by a refusal.'

She stared at the bit of steak on the end of her fork, and put it down. Suddenly she wasn't hungry any more.

Chelsea watched as Nick carefully teed up a golf ball on the ninth hole. 'This is a nice course,' he said as he stepped back to take an experimental swing.

Chelsea waited till he had made his drive, and watched the ball as it bounced off the edge of a sand trap and on towards the green. 'And you are a lucky golfer,' she grumbled as they walked towards the women's tee. She set up her shot, uncomfortably aware that Nick's bright eyes weren't missing a detail of the tailored white shorts she was wearing. If I have to spend much more time around this man, she thought, I'm going to reduce my wardrobe to trench coats and tent dresses.

'Why? Just because you're six shots down doesn't

mean I'm lucky,' Nick protested. 'Perhaps I'm just a better golfer.'

'You aren't even using your own clubs, for heaven's sake,' Chelsea protested.

'Doesn't that illustrate my point?'

'And you're just a bit conceited, too.'

'Who, me?' Nick asked innocently. 'Why do you leave your clubs here, by the way? St Louis has golf courses too, you know.'

'When do I ever get a chance to use them?'

'That's true,' he mused. 'Most of your leisure time must be tied up with Burke, and he hardly seems the type for golf.'

His bland assumption made her so furious that her swing was jerky, and her ball sailed off into the little pond at the bottom of the hill, landing with a splash that seemed to echo over the course. Chelsea stood there for a moment and looked down the slope. Then, maintaining her dignity with all the control at her command, she turned to face him. 'I'll concede the hole,' she said coolly.

'Very well,' Nick said equably. 'That's the same as conceding the game, you know. Too bad I was cautious about using your father's clubs. I might have won something from you.'

'It wouldn't have been much,' Chelsea snapped.

'Why? Aren't you sure enough of yourself to bet?' Nick put her club back in the bag strapped to the golf cart. 'Care to try another nine holes?'

'No, thanks.'

'Afraid I'll beat you again?'

'All that match proved was that you're a better heckler than I am, Nick.'

He looked wounded. 'I never heckle,' he said. 'Unless, of course, there's something worth winning at the end of the match. It looks to me as if you're sadly out of practice.'

'That was my first round of the year, yes.'

'Let's take your clubs back with us. Maybe we can do something about that.'

'I think they'll be fine right here.' She smiled at the boy who came out of the pro shop to take care of the cart and bags. 'I think the crowd has started to gather down by the pool. I understand that you may be uncomfortable, Nick. If you don't want to be dragged into it, that's fine with me. After all, you don't know any of the people, and . . .'

'I know you,' he offered.

'Well, it can't be a comfortable evening for you . . .'

'How sweet of you to worry about my comfort, Chelsea,' he said, and before she could dodge he'd put an arm around her waist, pulling her close to his side. 'I couldn't be rude and walk out on you when you've gone to such trouble to make me comfortable this weekend.'

Chelsea was still trying to find an answer to that when they reached the bottom of the little knoll. A knot of people had already gathered around the umbrella-shaded tables, and the scent of roasting pork drifted down from the barbecue pit.

'Besides, I never miss a meal if I can help it,' Nick continued, 'and since you're paying for this one——'

'I no longer owe you,' Chelsea snapped. She tried to pull away from his possessive arm, but he merely tightened his grip and smiled.

'Surely you don't mind being a security blanket, of a sort?' he asked. 'You're right, I don't know anyone but you. And I wouldn't want to get lost.'

Chelsea thought briefly about telling him where to go, but just then a cry went up from the tables. 'Chelsea! Where have you been, you scamp? You haven't been to a reunion in years!'

'We haven't had one in years,' she parried, as she was swallowed up by the group. Nick let his arm drop casually, and Chelsea breathed a quick sigh of relief, but then she found her hand captured in his in a grip that promised not to loosen all evening.

'And who's this?' one of the girls asked.

'I'm Nick Stanton,' he said with that easy smile. 'Chelsea brought me home on approval.'

Chelsea's teeth clenched. I'm going to make him regret that remark if it's the last thing I do, she swore.

It seemed hours later that she finally found herself alone. Dinner was long over, and the women had gathered under the umbrellas to gossip while the men clustered around the keg of beer at the far end of the terrace. Chelsea found her eyes resting on Nick's white shirt, clearly visible even in the dusk. She watched the muscles play under the close-fitting material, and then told herself not to be silly.

'Mooning over him? You'll get over it, once you've been married a couple of years.' The young woman who sat down next to her waved a hand towards the men.

'Hi, Janice. No, as a matter of fact, I'm not planning to be married at all.'

'That's smart. Next time I'm going to do the same.'

'Next time?' Chelsea asked idly.

Janice nodded. 'I'm on my second now. He's the one right by the beer keg. He's always right next to the keg, or the bar, or whatever's handy.'

'Do I know him?'

'No, but you know my first husband. He's over there too. That been a long time, though—six years and two kids ago.'

Chelsea propped her chin on her hand. The two men near the keg suddenly gave a roar of laughter. 'They seem to get alone fine.'

'Oh, they do. They play golf together every Sunday morning,' Janice said. Her voice was bitter. 'All I say is, don't trust 'em. Especially the handsome ones. And that one of yours is handsome as the very devil.'

It wasn't quite the way Chelsea would have stated it, but she couldn't help feeling that Janice's comparison was apt. Nick not only looked like the devil's first cousin, he was just as unpredictable. 'He isn't mine, actually. He's only my boss.'

Janice nodded sagely. 'Married, right? They all are.'

Chelsea was taken aback for a moment. Then she said slowly, 'Even if he was, it wouldn't make any difference to me. We're here this weekend to work, that's all.'

Nick leaned over the back of her chair and said, 'Want to go for a moonlight swim, Chels?'

'No, thanks. It's too soon after I ate.'

He shrugged. 'All right.' He planted a swift kiss on the nape of her neck and was gone.

Janice raised a knowing eyebrow. 'Your boss, hmmm? And you're here to work? Sure, Chelsea.'

I'm going to kill him, Chelsea thought. As slowly and as painfully as possible.

The sun was hot on Chelsea's bare back as she lay beside the pool. It was Sunday afternoon, and she was drowsing as she let the suntan oil begin to work.

Her mother fussed as she stood beside the lounger. 'Chelsea, you're going to roast out here,' she warned. 'And then you'll look awful in that new dress I got you.'

'Mother,' Chelsea said indistinctly, 'I will lie here no more than fifteen minutes. And I'm basted like a turkey; I can't possibly burn.'

'Well, be sure you move into the shade before you ruin that lovely skin.' Sara fussed with the spaghetti strap at the neckline of Chelsea's swimsuit. 'Don't you want this untied, honey? It will leave a line in your tan.'

'Mom, you're a dreamer to think that fifteen minutes of sun will give me a tan. Just go to your party and have a good time.'

'I hate to leave you, Chelsea. If it wasn't that the bride's father is one of Josh's best clients, we wouldn't feel so obligated to go to this reception. But . . .'

'Please go, Mother.' Chelsea closed her eyes.

'Well, I'll ask Nick to keep an eye on you and make sure you don't go to sleep out here.'

'I've sunbathed for twenty years without Nick's help, Mom. I think I can get through the day.'

'Nevertheless, it's a good precaution. You'll probably be over at the Bradley's by the time we get home, so we'll see you there for cocktails this evening, dear.'

'Goodbye, Mom.'

She heard the door slam and the engine of her father's car start, and sighed with relief. Her mother had the best of intentions, but sometimes she could drive Chelsea crazy. And it didn't help that for the last two days Sara had been telling her what a wonderful person Nick was.

What was really infuriating, Chelsea thought, was that he had been charming every moment that Josh and Sara were in view. It was only when they weren't around that the cynical side of him showed.

She lay there in the warmth and thought about Nick and what she'd like to tell him. What was there about that man, she wondered, that could arouse her to anger so quickly? Why could she not just ignore him? But the words she was planning to say kept getting all tangled together in her mind. And Nick kept coming into her head, with that easy smile and those expressive eyebrows, seeming to read her thoughts . . .

She stirred, hazily aware that she had slept. Oh, my God, she thought, I'll be burned so badly I won't be able to move. But the back of her neck, when she laid an experimental hand on it, was cool and supple. She looked up at the umbrella that stood over her, sheltering her from the blazing sun.

'So you're finally awake. I thought you'd never rejoin the conscious world, so I pulled the umbrella over.'

She looked over at the lounge drawn up next to hers. It was still in the sun, and Nick lay there in swimming trunks with an old copy of ARCHITECTURAL DIGEST in his hand.

'Don't you ever stop working?' she complained, and started to sit up before she remembered that her mother had untied her neck strap after all. Chelsea caught the top of her swimsuit just as it started to slide.

'Pity,' Nick mused, his gaze resting on the brief bikini top.

Chelsea's deep embarrassed blush seemed to start at her toes and spread over every inch of delicate skin.

'It must be very uncomfortable, being a redhead,' he mused. 'That luscious complexion doesn't let you keep any secrets.'

Chelsea was re-tying the straps and trying to ignore his watchful eyes.

'It's sweet of you to concern yourself about me, by the way,' he said, and tossed the magazine aside. 'Actually, I don't consider this work. I wondered once if I was a workaholic, but since I don't enjoy anything else as much as I like my job, I decided I must not be.' He looked at her, bright-eyed. 'But why do you ask? Do you have some other form of entertainment in mind?'

'Only swimming,' Chelsea retorted. She plunged into the pool and was halfway across when he broke the surface of the water right beside her.

He shook the water out of his and said, 'Want to play hide and seek? You can be IT.'

'In a pool this size? There's nowhere to hide.'

'That's why I want to play.' He grinned. 'You could at least say thank you. I saved you a nasty burn.'

'Thanks.' Chelsea started for the side of the pool.

'That wasn't quite the sort of appreciation I had in mind.' He came after her, his powerful stroke making her look helpless in the water.

'Oh? What did you mean?' Chelsea asked warily, treading water and trying to stay away from him.

'This might do,' he said softly. Then, suddenly, his arms were around her, her body was held firmly against his, and the warmth of his skin scorched her. 'Just a nice kiss,' he whispered.

'One kiss?' Chelsea was feeling slightly breathless. You're a little old for games in the swimming pool, she told herself, and then thought, what harm can it do? Play along, Chelsea—one kiss and then you can laugh the whole thing off. Fight him, and he'll keep bothering you.

He nodded solemnly, and then there was no more choice, for his mouth was warm and firm on hers. The combination of sensual stimuli—the burning pressure of his kiss, the slickness of the cool water as it lapped against her body, the heat of his skin and the tautness of his muscles under her hands—made her almost dizzy.

She was helpless in his arms, and the warmth of his skin seemed to burn through the nylon wisps of her swimsuit. I might as well be naked, she thought with the last thread of sense, and gave herself up to the pleasure of his embrace.

His hands were restless, exploring her body, stroking the delicate skin. His fingers struggled briefly with the wet ties of her bikini top, and then her breasts were free as the swimsuit floated away.

Chelsea gasped, and stretched out a hand to retrieve the flimsy top. But Nick silenced her with a kiss and captured her reaching fingers in his. 'No,' he breathed against her lips. 'Don't be shy, Chelsea. Don't hide from me.'

She swallowed hard as his hand gently cupped her breast, his thumb toying with the taut nipple. The sensation that shot through her was like an electric shock.

My God, what are you doing, Chelsea? The

question echoed through her mind, and she felt for a moment as if she had screamed it. She didn't even like this man, and yet she was allowing him to kiss her, and touch her, and play with her . . .

In sudden panic she pulled away and struck out for the edge of the pool.

Nick was only seconds behind her, pulling himself from the water before she had even collected her thoughts. Before she had taken two steps towards the house, he reached out for her. Her breasts were crushed against his chest and his hands rested on the curve of her hips as he held her close against him. 'I have to agree,' he said softly, and his lips brushed her wet cheek. 'The pool is fine for playing, but when it comes to serious lovemaking . . .'

Chelsea could barely breathe. 'You heel,' she spluttered. 'You low-down, rotten scum! Let me go!'

Nick tightened his grip. 'What's happened, Chelsea?' he asked, his voice taut. 'You were with me every step of the way. You wanted me just as much as I want you.'

'That's not true,' she denied hotly.

He raised a doubting eyebrow. 'Shall we test the theory?' he asked, and bent his head to kiss her again.

Chelsea tried to wriggle out of his arms, and succeeded only in arousing him further. 'You adorable, changeable little redhead,' he said. 'How I look forward to taming you!'

She gathered every ounce of strength she possessed and shoved him away. He lost his balance on the brink of the pool and tumbled in. Chelsea didn't stay to savour her triumph; she fled towards the house.

Confusion and relief were warring in her head as she reached her room and closed the door gratefully behind her. She sank on to the bench in front of her dressing table and stared at herself in the mirror.

'What is the matter with you, Chelsea Ryan?' she asked aloud.

'Damned if I know,' came a tart voice from the door.

She wheeled around, flinging up an arm to cover her bare breasts. 'Get out of here! Can't you even act like a gentleman?'

Nick leaned insolently against the door jamb. 'I was just informed that I'm a heel,' he told her. 'So I don't feel obligated to follow the gentleman's code.' He held up the dripping top of her swimsuit. 'I thought you might like to have this back, by the way.'

'Give it to me.'

'Why don't you come and get it?' he invited.

She stared at him for a long moment. The brief dark blue trunks hid little of his long tanned body as he stood there, the dark mat of hair on his chest still beaded with water. He was silently and defiantly male as he leaned against the door, arms folded, the scrap of green nylon dangling from his hand.

'Burke must be quite a guy,' he speculated. 'Or else, if I'm right about him, you're afraid to try your luck with a real man. I don't understand you, Chelsea. I have just as much power in the firm as Burke does. And I'm much younger and a whole lot more fun in bed.'

'You have a lot of confidence in yourself, don't you?' she jibed.

'I'd be delighted to let you form your own opinion,' Nick said silkily.

'I have no intention of finding out what you're like in bed. Ever.'

'You'd better be careful about making sweeping statements like that, Chelsea,' Nick mused. 'It tempts a man so.'

'Give me my swimsuit and go away,' Chelsea ordered.

Nick held up the swimsuit top and inspected it. 'I don't think I'll give it back after all,' he mused. 'Just a little souvenir of Norah Springs ... You wouldn't deny me that much, would you? I'll treasure it forever.' He tucked the scrap of fabric into the band of his trunks as if it was a scalp, waved a gentle hand, and vanished down the hall.

'I think it would be wonderful if the new civic centre had a bell tower.'

'A bell tower? Whatever are you thinking of, Elise?'

'I've seen them,' Elise Bradley defended her idea. 'They're lovely, really they are, with the bells pealing out over the city. It's a wonderful memorial.'

Chelsea tried to suppress a shudder, and said a silent prayer of thanks that George Bradley, and not Elise, was the one donating the civic centre to Norah Springs.

'So if you want a bell tower in your memory, leave the money in your will,' the other woman said bluntly. 'Bells on the civic centre! The idea, Elise!'

Chelsea finished her martini and set the glass aside. This had not been a good idea, she thought moodily; George should have had better sense than to turn the design of his civic centre over to a committee. If they actually incorporated all the suggestions that she had heard tonight, the place would look like a Rube Goldberg invention. And if they didn't, there would be a war in Norah Springs.

There was no point in her even being at the party anyway, she thought crossly. It would be Nick's project from start to finish; why should she even be involved in it? After the events of this afternoon, she would certainly have no influence on Nick.

But Chelsea was still caught in the crossfire. She smiled at another member of George's committee, and listened politely to yet another set of ideas, nodding once in a while. Then she looked up and found Nick's eyes resting on her from across the room. She felt suddenly very exposed in the backless black dress, and she turned away quickly and said something to the committee member that had nothing to do with his question.

Damn Nick Stanton anyway, she thought defiantly as she sipped another martini. All he had to do was look at her and she was uncomfortably aware that he knew precisely what she looked like without that basic black dress. She'd have worn something less revealing, except that her mother would have been disappointed if Chelsea had turned down the new dress. And, to tell the truth, she admitted, it wouldn't have made any difference what she was wearing. Nick would still have looked through it, as he was doing right now, making her feel absolutely naked in the middle of a crowd.

'You look as if a breath of fresh air would do you good.' The committee member had moved off and Nick appeared beside her.

'I don't want fresh air.'

'But I do.' His hand rested gently on the small of her back, seeming to burn an imprint on the bare skin. 'So let's go have a professional chat.'

'Strictly professional?'

'Cross my heart.'

'Well, I don't believe you. I think I'll stay right here.'

Nick shrugged. 'Have it your way. Do you know how beautiful you are tonight, by the way?'

'Yes. My mother told me.'

'Mothers don't count,' he said softly.

'I thought this was going to be a professional chat.'

'It would have been if you'd come outside. But since you decided to stay here . . .'

'You're going to tease me.' Chelsea tried to keep her voice steady.

'Oh, I'm not teasing. I believe every word I'm saying. You deserve to be told how beautiful you are out on the patio, in the moonlight, by your lover . . .'

'If I get desperate, I'll let you know.'

'You do that, darling,' he suggested, and his voice was a sensual caress. 'I'll be there.'

'Don't hold your breath, Nick.'

'Let me know when you change your mind, Chelsea.' He brushed a gentle finger down one tendril of auburn hair, and somehow the simple gesture became charged with sexuality. 'Remember that I never give up. I'll just keep rewriting the rules till you find a set you like, and eventually, you'll give in. You know it as well as I do.'

CHAPTER EIGHT

THE city sparkled under the afternoon sun, but Chelsea could almost see the heat waves bearing down on the concrete ten storeys below her office window. And some seventh sense deep inside her could feel the vibrations of the building as the cooling system struggled to keep the inside temperature down.

It is so early in the summer for it to be so hot, she thought moodily as she pushed the weight of her auburn hair up off her neck. Even air conditioning can't really fight the heat. She thought longingly of Norah Springs, of the shaded gallery, and a tall glass of freshly-squeezed lemonade . . . or the cool water in the pool . . .

She pushed her chair back from the desk with a motion so violent that it almost tipped over. Her face was flaming with the very memory of that pool as she strode across the room and stared out over the city.

'You're trying to hide, Chelsea,' she told herself glumly.

It had been three days since she and Nick had come back from Norah Springs, three days packed with hard work as they struggled with designs for the Jonas Building. The long, lazy weekend might have never been. She was just as overworked and exhausted now as she had been before the brief vacation.

Nick was a slave-driver, she thought, and then conceded that she too had been pushing hard on the project. She was in a hurry to have it done; there were too many other things to do . . .

'That's not true,' she told herself slowly. There was always other work waiting, but that wasn't why she was devoting so many hours to the Jonas Building.

She was pushing herself because she wanted to do her best work for Nick, to impress him with her ability.

What was happening to her? She was so confused that she didn't even know what she wanted any more. She did know that she wanted more from life than this unending race from project to project. She was tired of working from early morning till late at night, and then returning to an apartment where the only evidence of another human being was Judy's clothes scattered over the furniture. There was not so much as a goldfish that depended on her, that cared what happened to Chelsea Ryan.

There had to be more to life than that. Surely somewhere in the world was a person with whom she could share her life. There was such a thing as lasting, romantic marriage—her parents had found it, and Burke and Helen Marshall. Surely, somewhere, there was a man for her.

And you're least likely to find him when you're looking so hard, she scolded herself. It would be better by far to be alone than to be trapped in a loveless marriage, to be like Janice at the reunion who was married for the second time and already looking for a way out. No, that was far from what Chelsea wanted.

'You need a real vacation,' she told herself. Three days in Norah Springs had left her with only a taste of peace and quiet and relaxation, not enough to do any good. Perhaps if she could get away from everything for a while, she could regain her sense of humour. Away from the office, and the work piled high ... away from Nick ...

Was Nick what she wanted? The question seemed to echo deep in her mind. 'Don't be silly,' she told herself firmly, but the question wouldn't go away. What had happened to her there in the pool was unlike anything Chelsea had ever felt before. She had been no prude, even in high school, but never had she allowed herself to be so abandoned, so ... She put her hands to her hot cheeks, and tried not to think about Nick.

Nick——! The weekend might have never happened to him, either, from the way he had behaved since their return. He was polite, but preoccupied, and Chelsea was confused. He'd almost ignored her for the last few days. Had she, after all, only imagined those stunningly sensual moments in the pool?

'Well, I know I didn't imagine that threat at the cocktail party,' she told herself aloud. He had told her in no uncertain terms that he would continue to make passes at her until she gave in. But he hadn't. In the last three days he'd done nothing that wasn't exactly what she would expect from an employer . . .

And she was disappointed.

Chelsea's eyes widened in shock as the realisation hit her, and she groped for support, her hand clenching on the back of her chair. She dropped weakly into it.

She was disappointed that he had become the perfect gentleman. She had been enjoying the innuendo, the subtle teasing, the sensual byplay . . .

He had set a trap for her, and she had almost fallen into it, she realised. Anger swept over her. The sudden change in his behaviour had kept her off balance, made her wonder if she really did want him after all. And he had planned it that way, had schemed and plotted and probably enjoyed watching her confusion. He was waiting for her to come back and beg him to pay attention to her again!

Well, he would pay for that insolence, she was determined. And as she thought about it, a little smile crossed her face, and the big green eyes sparkled. She drew a wicked little sketch on a bit of scatch paper— Nick, wearing an explorer's pith helmet, sitting in a big iron pot, up to his neck in steaming water.

She shredded the drawing and hid it at the bottom of her wastebasket, and made a promise to herself. If

Nick Stanton thought he was going to have it all his own way, he would soon find out differently.

'May I come in, Chelsea?'

'Hi, Burke.' She looked up from the drawing board, feeling almost disappointed to see him. Surely sometime today Nick had to show up. She didn't want to go in search of him; it would fit much better into her plans if he came to her.

'Do you have the house plans here?' Burke closed her office door behind him. 'Helen and I were talking about it last night.'

Chelsea reached into the bottom drawer of her desk. 'They're pretty rough so far,' she warned, and handed him the roll of paper. 'How is Helen feeling?'

'Fair, these days. She misses you, by the way.'

Chelsea groaned. 'I know, Burke. I promise, I'll get out to see her this weekend.'

'Sorry. I didn't mean to make you feel guilty, Chelsea. Helen knows you're busy.' He spread the drawings out on the board.

'Do you have a site in mind?' Chelsea asked, leaning over his shoulder to help hold the drawings down.

'It will have to be almost perfectly level, won't it?'

'Not really. The design is adaptable. Is she seriously thinking about giving up Hillhaven now?'

He nodded. 'It's increasingly harder for her to move around. Helen's no fool.'

Chelsea bit her lip. 'How long does she have?' she asked quietly. 'Before she can't walk at all, I mean.'

There was a tap at the door, and Nick put his head in just as Burke said, 'I think the doctors were generous when they said six months, Chelsea. She's getting weaker by the day.'

'Sorry to interrupt this important conference,' Nick said. His tone was cheery, but his eyes snapped as they rested on Chelsea, who was still leaning over Burke's shoulder. 'Will you be able to see me a little later?'

'Come back in half an hour,' Chelsea said.

Nick didn't take the hint. He came across the room. 'New project, Burke?'

'Just a . . .'

Chelsea firmly cut across the sentence. 'Nothing important, Nick.' Her quelling look silenced Burke, and she rolled the plans up again so that Nick couldn't get a look at them.

He looked through her. 'I'll see you in thrity minutes, Chelsea.'

The door hadn't completely closed behind him when Burke leaned back in his chair, tented his fingers together, and said, 'What's up, Chelsea? Why didn't you want Nick to see the house plans?'

'Because the house doesn't have anything to do with the office, that's why. It's strictly a free-lance project, and it's none of his business.'

Burke looked thoughtful, but he didn't push the matter.

Chelsea didn't give him a chance to ask more questions. She spread the plans out again and picked up a pencil. 'I just took a guess on size. I don't imagine Helen will be entertaining as much.'

'That's a safe bet.' He studied the drawings. 'The kitchen looks really strange.'

'I know. But it follows the best advice available. They took a bunch of architecture students at one of the universities and put them in wheelchairs for a week. It drove them crazy, but at the end of the week they had come up with the handicap-free kitchen. This is it, with a few modifications of my own.'

'Hmmm. Want to bring these over this weekend and talk to Helen?'

'You can take them with you if you like.'

'I'd rather you came over.' Burke let the drawings curl up into a loose roll. 'You can do a better sales job than I could.'

'Burke . . .' Chelsea's voice was hesitant. 'If Helen is going downhill so rapidly . . .'

'What, Chelsea?'

'Can we even have the house built in time?'

'We can hurry it along, and by the time she's confined to the wheelchair . . .'

'That wasn't what I meant, Burke.' Chelsea's voice was gentle. 'This is a progressive disease, and it isn't just crippling. It's a killer.'

He sighed heavily. 'I know. It may just be another worry to her, and pointless in the end. But it might also give her a new interest, something to look forward to. I think Helen has to make the choice.'

'You're right, of course.' Chelsea put the drawings away. 'I'll come this weekend.'

'How was your holiday? I've barely seen you since you came back.'

'Norah Springs was wonderful. Since then, we've been working on the Jonas Building. It's soaking up all my time.'

'That's what I heard. Stanton and Ryan, together again.'

Chelsea's heart did a strange little flip-flop.

'You really ought to stop fighting with the man, you know, Chelsea. Everybody who has seen the Sullivan house agrees that you do better work together than either of you can alone.'

'I know.' Her tone was sarcastic. 'It's one of the seven wonders of the world.'

This time Nick didn't bother to tap on the door. When he came in, Chelsea lost her temper. 'Dammit, Nick, would you learn to knock?' she snapped.

'I did make an appointment,' he pointed out. But his expression dared her to remember another time, and another door, and Chelsea fought to keep herself from blushing at the memory of sitting in her bedroom in half a swimsuit with Nick lounging in the doorway and enjoying the view. She found herself wondering just what he had done with the top of her bikini.

Burke stood up. 'I'll leave you to your work. See you this weekend, then, Chelsea.'

'Saturday afternoon?'

'That would be fine.'

Nick waited till the door had clicked shut. 'So you're making dates. I always thought the chief advantage of affairs was that you never had to plan ahead.' He frowned. 'Or is it the other way round?'

'Do you really care?'

'No. I'm sure you understand all the fine details, and that's all that is necessary.'

'Then shall we get to work?'

'Certainly. What in the hell is this?' He was leaning over her drawing board.

'It's a bathroom. You've probably drawn a few in your day.'

'Not like this one. It looks more like a massage parlour. Where are the specs?'

'Oh, come on, Nick. I'm not even finished designing it yet and you want specifications?'

'You have them somewhere or you couldn't draw the darn thing.' He snapped his fingers. 'Hand them over, Chelsea.'

Reluctantly, she did. He scanned the pamphlet and looked up in shock. 'You're putting in contoured bathtubs? What's wrong with the old kind, for heaven's sake?'

'From you, of all people, I expected a little creativity,' Chelsea snapped. 'A standard bathtub is dangerous and uncomfortable.'

'Also cheap,' Nick pointed out.

'Which the condos in the Jonas Building are certainly not going to be, so why not put in a safe tub? Five hundred dollars more for a comfortable one . . .'

'Per tub?'

'Yes,' she admitted.

'Times a hundred bathrooms makes fifty thousand dollars. We could build another whole unit for that.'

'We could not. And we don't need a hundred, anyway. I'm standing firm, Nick. I'm tired of building bathrooms for the convenience of the plumber, instead of the owner. The tub is contoured for proper support of the spine . . .'

Nick grunted. 'You take a lot of bubble baths, don't you?'

'Yes.' Chelsea refused to be disturbed. 'And so do a lot of other people. Taking a bath should be a sensual experience.'

He grinned suddenly. 'In that case, let's put in bathtubs built for two!'

Chelsea fought the blush, and lost. 'Whirlpools are standard in those tubs. That's included in the price.'

'I'm charmed.' He didn't sound it. 'While we're talking about surprises in store for the new owner, I'm sure you have done something to the all-American shower.'

'Nothing.'

He quirked an eyebrow. 'A bit discriminatory, aren't you?'

Chelsea gave in. 'All right. But all I did was add an extra shower head, lower, so you don't have to get your hair wet if you don't want. And . . .'

'Where do you plan to cut back expenses to balance these extravagances?'

Chelsea lost her temper. 'Obviously you've never shared a bathroom in a modern apartment block or you wouldn't call six extra square feet an extravagance!'

'Does Burke take up a lot of room?' he asked interestedly.

Chelsea bit her tongue, clenched her fists, counted to ten, and still wanted to hit him. Then she remembered the plans she had made earlier in the afternoon, and slowly she relaxed her grip and smiled, a sweet, charitable smile. 'You asked me to design the condos,' she reminded him. 'If you've changed your mind . . .'

'Oh, of course not. You're the expert, after all.' He walked slowly across the room towards her, and stopped just inches away. His voice was a slow caress as he said, 'I'd love to have you teach me all you know about . . . everything. Tell me, Chelsea, have you changed your mind?'

'Are you asking me about the condos or the affair?' she asked tartly.

'Affair?' he asked innocently. 'I'm sorry to disappoint you, Chelsea, but I never discuss intimate matters like that in the office. If you'd like to have dinner with me tonight, though . . .'

She didn't look up at him; she was afraid if she did he would see the gleam of amusement in her eyes. So she kept her gaze demurely downcast and said, letting just a wisp of uncertainty creep through, 'Perhaps we should get this all straightened out, Nick. The Sullivans are coming in at six to talk about their house plans, but after that we could go somewhere quiet. What about Top of the Tower? Shall I call for reservations?'

He looked suspicious. 'Are we suitably dressed?'

'As long as you wear a jacket they'll let you in. But if you'd like to change clothes, you can pick me up at home on your way.' She raised innocent green eyes to his.

'I don't trust you as far as I can throw you, Chelsea Ryan. I'll make the reservations.'

'Why, Mr Stanton, I'm shocked that you'd say such a thing to a lady.'

'As a matter of fact,' he smiled suddenly, 'I wouldn't. But then, you aren't a lady. What about the rest of the condos? Is there anything else we need to argue about?'

*　　*　　*

The Top of the Tower was the best-known restaurant in the city, located in one of the classic old hotels. Strictly speaking, the restaurant was not the top, because the penthouses were above it, and at ten stories, it scarcely qualified as a tower. But the name had stuck.

And, what was far more important to Chelsea, the place had a reputation for serving the best food at the most prohibitive price in the entire state. It was the ideal opening gun in her campaign to get even with Nick Stanton.

She adjusted the spaghetti strap of her midnight blue dinner dress and looked down at Judy, who was curled up on the couch, with a frown.

'Sorry about the summer cold,' Judy said, and sneezed. 'Believe me, it doesn't fit into my plans any better than it does yours. I just hope I can shake it before the weekend. I don't want to meet Jim's aunt and uncle with a red nose and watery eyes.'

'They'll love you,' Chelsea said automatically. 'But make sure you disappear into your room by the time we get back.'

'Oh, I will. I think you're crazy, Chels, and I want nothing to do with this escapade. I'm actually sorry I didn't go to work.' She watched Chelsea step into the highest-heeled shoes in her closet. 'Make sure you take your charge card.'

'Why on earth should I?'

'Because if your plans go wrong and you get stuck with the bill, it would take years to wash enough dishes to pay it off,' Judy warned.

'I'll just call you to rescue me.'

'Don't bother. I don't get paid till tomorrow, and right now I don't have a dime.' Judy scooped up her blanket and box of tissues. 'I shall now retire until after Sir Galahad has swept you off.'

'I think you have the wrong knight.'

'Perhaps, but I know you do. You are going to regret this stunt.'

Chelsea shrugged. 'I might. But Nick Stanton certainly will, and that's perfectly good enough for me.'

'Why don't you stay home and we'll mix up an oatmeal facial and catch up on the gossip? I haven't talked to you since I went on the afternoon shift.'

Chelsea just shook her head. 'No. I'm determined to do this.'

The doorbell rang just as Judy disappeared down the hall into her bedroom, and Chelsea took a deep breath and crossed the living room to answer it.

You're going to get along with him tonight if it kills you, Chelsea, she reminded herself firmly. At least till the end of the evening. And then——!

She flirted with him throughout dinner. At first she felt self-conscious and a tiny bit guilty, but after a few moments of wary surprise, Nick seemed happy enough to play along. Chelsea ate her steak and lobster with delighted unconcern for what the bill would total. To Nick's credit, he didn't seemed worried either. He merely kept her wine glass filled and the conversation going on one light topic after another.

The only time it got serious was when Chelsea brought up the Sullivans. 'I didn't think they were going to accept the house,' she said. 'There was a moment when Doris was explaining why none of their friends liked it, and I thought she was going to turn it down altogether.'

Nick shrugged. 'They're pretty conventional people. And you have to admit that's a very unconventional house.'

Chelsea dug the last bite of meat out of her lobster tail. 'But it's so beautiful.'

He shook his head. 'To people like the Sullivans, it isn't a matter of beauty. That house is simply outside their ability to understand.'

'To say nothing of the difficulty with her brother. I told you that man thought he was an expert. I still can't believe he told them they ought to stick to a ranch-style for the resale value!' She shook her head in disbelief.

'You did a marvellous job convincing them to go ahead, Chelsea.'

'I'm certain they'll love it, once it's built.'

'Perhaps. But even if they change their minds, we'll still build that house, Chelsea.'

The easy assumption that their partnership would continue caught at Chelsea's throat.

'Someone else will appreciate it,' Nick went on, 'probably far more than the Sullivans are capable of.'

'They are going to love it,' Chelsea said firmly. 'But let's stop being serious, Nick. This is a night for fun.'

'My thinking exactly.' He reached for her hand. 'Are you ready to go?'

Chelsea felt just a little breathless. 'Before dessert? The pineapple torte here is wonderful.'

'I have no doubt it is.' He was smiling, just a little, and for a moment Chelsea wondered uneasily if she ought to call the whole thing off. But the waiter brought the dessert trolley by just then, so she told herself firmly that nothing was wrong; she was still in perfect control of the situation. She toyed with her dessert for a long time before finally pushing the plate aside. 'It's late, Nick.'

'You finally noticed?' But there was an undercurrent of amusement in his voice.

'Coffee at my apartment?' she asked, trying to sound casual.

Nick didn't even look at her. 'If you like.' He paid the bill with no more than a glance, which disappointed Chelsea, and spent a great deal of time draping her shawl just right around her shoulders. By the time they reached his car, she was feeling uneasy again. The brush of his hands up her bare back had been far from casual.

The night sky was like velvet as it lay over the city.

Nick took the indirect route back to her apartment, through Forest Park, Chelsea let her head rest against the back of the seat and watched dreamily as they passed the lagoons and fountains left from the turn-of-the-century world's fair. If she half-closed her eyes, she thought, she could almost see the ladies with their long skirts and parasols and hear the bustle of the crowd as they waited to ride the enormous observation wheel.

She was almost reluctant to have the ride end, and her heart was pounding as she climbed the stairs with Nick beside her. When he took the key from her fingers to unlock the apartment door, she was trembling.

Now, she thought. Now all you have to do is let him make a fool of himself, and then laugh at him. And then Nick Stanton will never bother you again . . .

When she would have turned on a light, he caught her hand and pulled her tight against him. 'It's pleasant to be the seduced instead of the seducer, Chelsea,' he murmured, his voice a sensuous whisper. He found her lips in the darkness, and took his time about kissing her, gently at first, and then with a growing hunger.

This was the weak spot of her plan, she knew, but she had gambled everything on being able to resist the awesome magnetic pull of his charm. Besides, she thought, what had happened in the pool that day had been the exception. It had been coincidence, and it couldn't happen again.

She was quickly disillusioned. She could not hold out against him; she simply didn't have enough strength. Her body was instinctively answering his demands, wanting him, begging for more. Then panic took hold of her mind, screaming at her to break away from him, to release herself from his arms no matter what the cost.

She tore herself away from him, gasping for breath

and feeling as if she had ripped herself in two. She reached for the nearest support, bracing her hands on a small table to hold herself upright. If he touches me, she thought, I will be finished.

'Are you having a few last doubts?' Nick asked softly. 'If you'd like, Chelsea, we could always have another contest. That might help you make up your mind.'

'Contest?' she asked breathlessly. It was the only word that seemed to make sense to her whirling brain.

'Yes. If I win, you go to bed with me. If you win— but you wouldn't, would you, darling?' His voice was as intimate as a touch could have been. 'Even if you had to lose on purpose, you would lose. Because this is what you want——'

Her hand found the switch on the table lamp. Fury burned in her veins now, and she turned on him like a wildcat. 'You really think you're something special, don't you, Nicholas Stanton?'

Nick's body tensed, and Chelsea's anger gave way to raw fear. Thank God, she thought, that Judy was in the next room . . .

With an effort, he relaxed, and reached out to touch her cheek. Chelsea shivered under the gentle fingers. If he tries to kiss me again, she thought, I can't say no. It's crazy, but I couldn't refuse him anything right now.

The telephone rang almost under her hand, and she picked it up. Before she could say anything, a tense, frantic voice said, 'Chelsea?'

She said, slowly, 'Burke? What is it?'

'Helen's ill. I'm at the hospital—they say she's had a stroke, Chelsea. She asked for you.'

'Which hospital?'

He told her. 'She may not make it through the night.'

'I'll be right there, Burke.' She put the phone down and stood there for an instant, her fingers still clenched on it.

'It's always Burke, isn't it? It will always be Burke.'
Nick's voice was quiet. 'I wish I understood why,
Chelsea.'

She turned slowly. 'Well, this time it isn't Burke.
It's Helen, and she may be dying.'

He stared at her for a long moment. Then his mouth
twisted. 'So the mistress is going to join the
deathwatch. Six months, I believe Burke said this
afternoon. Perhaps you won't have to wait so long
after all, Chelsea.' He turned on his heel. 'I'll be
leaving now. I wouldn't want to delay you.'

'Nick, it isn't that . . .' Chelsea's voice trailed off.
What point was there in trying to explain?

And at any rate, he was already gone.

Chelsea was late to work the next morning, and she
felt like yesterday's leftovers after a night at the
hospital. But at least Helen had hung on through the
long hours, and it looked much more positive in the
light of day.

Marie was looking particularly testy; she didn't even
say good morning before telling Chelsea that Mr
Stanton wanted to see her immediately.

Chelsea glanced at her watch and made a face. 'If
I'm already two hours late, it can't hurt to have a cup
of coffee, can it?' she asked, trying to sound
unconcerned.

Marie gave her a sour look and turned back to her
typewriter.

Chelsea took her time, straightening her hair,
picking up the designs that she had been working on
the previous afternoon. After all, she thought, that
might be all Nick was looking for—but she wasn't
convinced.

His secretary tapped on the heavy door and
announced her. Chelsea followed the girl in, doing her
best to look airily unconcerned.

Nick didn't bother to stand. He waved a hand

towards a chair and Chelsea sat down, straightening her white linen skirt.

'I brought the condo designs,' she said.

'Cut it out, Chelsea. You know damned well that you're not here to discuss condos.'

'Oh? Then what did you want to talk about?'

'Just what sort of game were you playing last night?'

Chelsea parried, 'I thought you never talked about things like that in the office.'

His eyes smouldered. 'That was yesterday, Chelsea, and now I want an answer. Were you planning to seduce me to cover up your affair with Burke, or just to see how big a fool I'd make of myself?'

She arched her foot and studied the curve of her instep in the high-heeled, strappy sandal. Then she looked up at him and said softly, 'I certainly had no plans to go to bed with you, Nick.'

He raised an eyebrow. 'And I played right into your hand, didn't I?' he said softly.

'It was rather amusing,' she agreed. Her voice was brittle.

'And yet, you weren't exactly untouched, my dear. Just how much longer do you think you'd have held out, if it hadn't been for Burke's call?'

About another thirty seconds, came the answer from the back of Chelsea's mind. She shrugged and tried to look unconcerned.

'How is Helen this morning, by the way?'

'Better. She's paralysed on one side—that may go away or it may last.'

'But she'll live.'

'Yes.'

'So you and Burke will have to wait after all. And I don't think you want to kick up a scandal right now.'

'What are you suggesting, Nick?' she asked coolly.

'That we have a little fun together in the meantime.'

'An affair?'

'That seems to be the standard terminology.'

'Why?' Chelsea asked baldly.

'I've grown fond of Helen in the last few weeks,' Nick said. His tone was casual, conversational. 'I'd like to do my part to make sure she dies in peace. If I'm in the picture, she certainly isn't going to be suspecting Burke.'

'How self-sacrificing of you.' Chelsea's voice was sweetly sarcastic.

'Oh, I think it will be worth my while. And I am still attracted to you.'

'Whoopee.'

'I know. Foolish of me, isn't it?'

'Are you certain you can afford me? I'm rather expensive.'

'Yes, I found that out last night. I think I can manage the price for a while.'

Chelsea held her temper with an effort. 'What if I don't . . . co-operate?'

'Carl Shelby will get a set of caricatures to hang on his office wall.'

She'd forgotten that he still had the drawings. Her throat was tight; it hurt to breathe.

'Funny,' Nick mused. 'I had them in the car last night. I was going to give them back to you.'

'We did have a bargain. The Jonas Building condos for the drawings. Remember?' Chelsea kept her voice steady with an effort.

'Of course I remember. But after last night, all deals are off.'

'You must be very desperate, Nick.' Chelsea stood up. 'I'm not interested. Do what you want with the drawings. Even if Shelby fires me, at least I'll be rid of you. But I warn you, Nick—don't bring Burke into it, or hurt Helen.'

She closed the door very quietly behind her and stood in the outer office for a moment. She wanted to run down the hall, or to burst into tears. But the secretary was there, and a client, reading a magazine as she waited. Lovely woman, Chelsea thought absently. Nick would like working with her; she was just his type. Dark and exotic, slim and elegant and probably very tall . . .

Nick's secretary looked up at Chelsea and then reached for the intercom button on her desk. 'Mr Stanton?' she said quietly. 'Mrs Stanton is here. Shall I show her in?'

CHAPTER NINE

CHELSEA'S first instinct was self-preservation. She ducked down the hall and was out of sight by the time Nick's office door opened. But she heard him say, 'Vanessa!' and the tone of his voice brought hot tears to her eyes.

What man wouldn't be delighted to have Vanessa Stanton waiting for him, she thought drearily. The woman was gorgeous—exquisite features, designer clothes . . .

And Nick was a lying, two-timing cheat! The fury that spread through her like a fever burned away the tears. He had a lot of nerve to accuse her of having an affair with Burke, when Nick himself was cheating on his wife.

But he didn't actually do anything immoral, Chelsea's conscience argued. She thought about that, and then shook her head. That didn't excuse Nick's behaviour, she told herself firmly. At the very least, he had been perfectly willing to start an affair with her, and in Chelsea's estimation, it added up to the same thing.

For that matter, she told herself forlornly, there probably were any number of other women in Nick's past. Stupid, she thought, to have imagined that there was something special about the chemistry between the two of them. Utterly stupid.

She had known perfectly well that women found Nick attractive. And vice-versa, too, she told herself cynically. So why was she so surprised that he had a wife?

But the grapevine hadn't known. She would swear that no one in the office knew he was married . . .

So the plans he'd given up for that holiday weekend

had included his wife. And when he couldn't spend the time with Vanessa, he had turned to Chelsea.

Her cheeks were burning by the time she reached the relative safety of her office. She closed the door firmly behind her and leaned against it with a sigh of relief. She wanted to barricade the furniture against the door and stay there, hidden in her burrow, forever. It would be easier if she never had to see him again . . .

'But you do have to face him,' she told herself firmly. 'And if you walk around the office looking like this, it will take about two minutes for the entire staff to know what happened.' The thought made her shudder. They no doubt knew about Vanessa already, and Chelsea would be just another titbit. The phony concern, the gossip behind her back—she could almost hear the vicious whispers now.

'Did you hear about Chelsea? She thought—the poor dear actually thought that Nick Stanton was serious about her. You should have SEEN her when she met his wife! . . .'

It would go on and on, passing from secretary to secretary, from department to department, until it would be impossible for Chelsea to hold up her head at Shelby Harris.

'I'll go home,' she said. Home to Norah Springs, and Mother, and that little office waiting for me . . .

But that would be no better. She might not have to listen to the gossip, but running away would not stop it. It might even fuel the fires of speculation.

'It must have been pretty serious if she ran away when his wife found out about them. I wonder if Nick paid her off. I wonder . . . I wonder . . .'

Chelsea shuddered. The gossip would be bad enough, but such an act would be professional suicide. She couldn't afford to leave Shelby Harris without giving notice and without any kind of reference. It would be hard enough to set up a practice in Norah Springs even if she had the firm's blessing and the recommendation of the partners. But the way it was, she would get no help at all to set up her own practice.

'I'm stuck,' Chelsea told herself fatalistically. 'I'm going to have to stay here and face it.'

No wonder all the experts preached that romance didn't belong in the office. The pain was too great for everyone when it didn't work out.

Of course, a little honesty would have helped, she thought. If Nick had just told her the truth, she would never have got into this mess. Then she jeered at herself. Silly, to expect honesty from a man who was determined to seduce her. If she hadn't been so innocent, she'd have suspected all along that he was married.

'You learned your lesson cheaply,' she told herself, keeping her voice firm. 'It didn't cost you anything but a lot of pride. So take the medicine and hide your hurt, and tomorrow will look brighter.'

It sounded good. She wondered unhappily if she could carry it out.

Her nerves were raw. She had managed to do a great deal of work in a couple of hours, but her hands were shaking and her concentration was gone. When Jim tapped on her door, Chelsea wanted to scream at him to stay out.

'Chelsea? I hate to question you, but . . .'

'What is it, Jim?'

He bit his lip. 'I know you're the architect and I'm only the draughtsman, but on these re-modelling plans that you gave me this morning . . .'

Get to the point, Jim, she wanted to yell. But she held on to the shreds of her sanity.

'Look at this, Chelsea. You knocked out a load-bearing wall, and you haven't reinforced it. The house will collapse if you actually do that.'

'Where?' He was right; she could scarcely believe herself that she had been so careless. 'Thanks, Jim.

I'm glad you spotted that.' Before it got to Nick, she thought. Nick would not have found the mistake humorous—or forgivable.

'Anytime. Hey, are you all right? You look really strange.'

'I'm sure some fresh air would do me good.' She finished off her cold coffee and set the crystal mug aside. 'I think I'll go out on the sites today.'

'Maybe it's just too much coffee. You've probably drunk a gallon of the stuff today.'

'Perhaps I have.' Chelsea didn't care.

'Have something to eat. That will help.'

She was, she found to her surprise, actually a little hungry. No sleep last night, no breakfast this morning ... No wonder she felt so awful. 'I'll do that, Jim. Thanks for caring.'

'Sure, Chelsea.' He sounded a little surprised.

Watch your step, she warned herself, and left a note on Marie's desk to tell her that she'd be out for the afternoon. She was silently thankful that the woman had gone to lunch; Marie seldom missed anything.

One mistake like that one getting past Jim and on to Nick, and Chelsea wouldn't need to worry about serving out her notice. She'd be fired on the spot, she thought morosely as she followed her favourite waiter to one of the secluded booths that were so popular at Angelo's. Nick would probably be delighted to have an excuse to get rid of her.

And then I'd go back to Norah Springs with one more strike against me, she thought. She moodily nibbled on a breadstick, grateful for the secluded corner where no one in the restaurant could see her. Chelsea didn't think she could maintain her poise if any of the girls from the office happened to come in and join her.

She'd try to eat something, and then she'd go out to the sites. It had been a week since she'd checked on them, and an afternoon of fresh air, warmth, and

solitude would do her good. Then when she had
checked on all of her projects, she'd stop to see Helen
at the hospital, and go home to catch up on her sleep.

That was why she had reacted so strongly to
Vanessa Stanton, she told herself. It had nothing to do
with Nick, at all, it was simply hunger and lack of
sleep. Feeling a little better about herself, she
munched another breadstick.

'It's a cute place, Nicky, but the calories . . .' The
low-pitched, sexy voice from the next booth caught
Chelsea's attention. 'I didn't know you were into
Italian food.'

'One of my colleagues recommended it.'

Nicky? Chelsea thought. The waiter put a plate of
fettucini before her, and she stared at it silently. So
she was a colleague now, was she? What else did you
expect, Chelsea? she asked herself sarcastically. He
wouldn't be likely to say, I brought a girl from the
office here and tried to seduce her.

Nick continued, his voice clipped, 'It wouldn't hurt
you to put on a few pounds, Vanessa.'

'The camera sees every ounce, Nick. I can't model if
I'm fat.'

'You? That would be a joke if we weren't talking
about a life being at stake here.'

'Oh, come on, Nick! It's not alive, it's hardly even a
lump of protoplasm yet. Would you come down out of
the pulpit now? You told me yourself two years ago
that you thought I'd make a terrible mother.'

'That's absolutely true.' Nick's voice was dry. 'I did
say that.'

'Now all of a sudden you're saying I should keep the
baby. Come on, Nick, be reasonable.'

'Abortion isn't a reasonable alternative, Vanessa.'

'So what am I supposed to do? If I go through with
this pregnancy, I'll be out of work for nearly a year.
By that time the style could change, and I might never
be able to work again, Nick. A cover girl doesn't have

a long career expectancy, you know, even without taking time off to have a baby.'

'I know.' Nick's voice was cold. 'But there are other people involved in this decision.'

'I don't see why. It's my body, and I want an abortion.'

Chelsea pushed the fettucini around on her plate and searched desperately for a way to avoid hearing this conversation. She couldn't just walk out; it was impossible to reach the entrance without Nick and Vanessa seeing her.

Vanessa said, 'You make sacrifices for your career, too, Nick. My God, you live in St Louis—that ought to be sacrifice enough for anyone.'

'The things you give up are entirely your choice, Vanessa. It's no one's business but yours if you stop eating pastry and chocolate bars. But it seems to me that the one doing all the serious sacrificing here is an innocent baby.'

'God, Nick, would you stop calling it a baby? You make it sound like I'm smothering some cute little bundle in a cradle!'

Chelsea gestured to the waiter. 'I'd like my bill, please,' she told him.

He looked horrified. 'But Miss! You have eaten nothing! Nothing!'

'I know. Just bring me the bill.' I can't take any more of this conversation, she thought.

Nick's quiet voice broke through her determination not to hear. 'I do have more than an abstract interest in this particular baby, Vanessa.'

Chelsea could take no more. She slid out of the booth and met her waiter halfway to the kitchen. 'Here,' she said, and thrust a twenty-dollar note into his hand. 'Keep the change. Is there a back entrance to this place?'

He looked down at the money in his hand, and Chelsea could almost see his brain working as he calculated the percentage of his tip. Then he looked up at her with a wink. 'Miss is avoiding someone?' he asked with a broad smile.

'Miss is certainly trying to,' Chelsea retorted.

'This way,' he said, gesturing confidentially, and turned to lead her through the kitchen.

Sorry, Angelo, she thought as she ducked her head to avoid the curious gazes of the aproned cooks, but I won't be coming back. I still love the food, but after today the atmosphere will never be the same.

The early heat wave had broken, and the day was as perfect as June could make it. The construction workers were making the most of the pleasant weather; most of them were stripped to the waist as they climbed like monkeys over the rapidly-growing framework of the house. The sharp scent of freshly-sawed wood, the piercing roar of the power tools, the rhythmic banging of the hammers tugged at Chelsea's senses as she parked the Mercedes at the curb and reached for her low heeled shoes.

Funny, she thought, how a house could look so big in the drawings, and then so very cramped when the site was staked out. But now, as the framework grew, the house would seem to expand again. It was one of the small joys that kept her fascinated with building houses.

The foreman saw her coming. 'Hi, Chelsea. Grab yourself a hard hat and come on in.'

She tucked the auburn waves of her hair up under the bright yellow plastic helmet and followed him in, ducking through the doorway. 'It's going fast,' she observed. She'd staked this house out only a few weeks ago.

He grinned and wiped a gloved hand across his brow to mop away the perspiration. 'We're in a hurry for the topping-off party.'

Chelsea's experienced eyes summed up the work. 'About another week to finish the framing, right?'

'Something like that. The owner's already talking change orders on the interior, by the way. He was out this morning with all kinds of grand ideas. I told him to call you.'

'What sort of changes?'

'Oh, the wife has decided she'd rather have casement windows. And the bathroom looked too small. I told him it was a bit late to do anything about that. That's the problem with amateurs, Chelsea.'

'I know. But what other kind of clients do I get?' She gave him a innocent smile. 'Everybody likes the houses I design so well that they never want to move again.'

The foreman groaned. 'Come on, Chelsea! We all know you're good, but that's spreading it on too thick.'

Chelsea shrugged. 'If no one else will say nice things about me, I'll have to do it myself.'

'Don't give me that garbage. I wasn't born yesterday. Hey, since you're here—will you interpret some drawings for me?'

It took the better part of an hour to straighten out all the details, and to answer all the questions that had popped up since her last visit. By the time she pulled the Mercedes back into traffic, Chelsea felt a little better. The concentration on the job she really loved, instead of on the office-bound paperwork that was so necessary, had brightened her outlook.

The next house was beautiful from the street. If it wasn't for the look of horrible emptiness conveyed by bare windows and scraps of wood scattered around the unfinished lawn, it would almost have looked complete. Only an electrician was at work, whistling out of tune as he installed light fixtures in the kitchen. Chelsea inspected the work, made a mental note to call the owner, and found the electrician taking a coffee break.

'We're ahead of schedule,' she said, leaning against the kitchen counter.

He nodded. 'Feels good for a change. Want a cup of coffee?'

Chelsea shook her head. 'Where are the rest of the guys today?'

'The contractor pulled them off here to start another job.'

Chelsea frowned. 'That's just great. When does he plan to finish this one?'

The electrician shrugged. 'You know how some of these big shots are sometimes. Unless they're running from job to job they don't think they're making any progress. He left some bills over there for you to approve.'

Chelsea looked at the bills, dog-eared and grimy from being moved around the construction site. She signed three of them, and left a note on the fourth that she'd be delighted to approve it except that the work it covered hadn't been done yet.

She still had trouble with contractors sometimes, she reflected. Some of them thought that because she was a woman they could get by with half-done jobs, or poor workmanship, or shoddy construction.

She wondered idly if Nick might have some suggestions for convincing the contractors that there were no short cuts with her. And then anger rose in her again as she remembered what Nick still thought of her, even after all this time—that she had won her present position by sleeping with Burke Marshall.

The contractors, Nick—all of them assumed that a woman architect had to be incompetent. It wasn't very smart of them, actually, to jump to that conclusion. After all, Chelsea had passed the same exams as any man to get her licence. In fact, she'd always thought her education was worth more than that of most of the men she'd gone to school with. She'd had to work ten times harder to convince her professors that she really wanted to be an architect, that she hadn't chosen the profession because—as the rare woman in the field—she could have a larger choice of men.

Men! They all thought alike, and Chelsea was tired of listening to them. Maybe we should start our own company, she thought. There were some good women carpenters around. A plumber here and there, an electrician ... A construction company composed entirely of women. Why not? They'd probably pay much better attention to details, she thought.

She glanced at her watch. Better stop playing with ideas and get to the hospital, she told herself. She hadn't talked to Burke all day.

But she found herself driving along the side streets instead, down the winding lanes of the suburb where the Sullivans had bought their land. There was nothing to be done there yet; she had talked them into continuing with the planning process, but until final plans were drawn and accepted there would be no work to be done at the site.

But Chelsea found herself parking the Mercedes at the corner of the lot anyway. She walked back over the hillside, kicking at the sticks and bits of debris that lay over the untended ground, visualising the house as it would appear. It would be fun to build that one, she thought.

The Sullivans were crazy if they didn't jump at the chance to build Nick's design. The sheer beauty of it brought a lump to Chelsea's throat as she thought about the house clinging to the steep hillside. But the Sullivans were conventional people, and they didn't see the sculptured beauty. They only saw that the house was different from everyone else's.

Funny, she thought, that at first they had wanted a male architect, and then when they got one, they didn't like his ideas.

Absently, Chelsea paced out the dimensions of the house. Right about here was where the kitchen would

be, she thought, and stopped to stare out across the
hillside at Doris Sullivan's view. She sat down on a
little patch of grass under the sunlight that streamed
through the trees, and relaxed. No one could find her
here; no one knew where to look. There was great
relief in knowing that no telephones could ring out
here.

A songbird began to sing, and Chelsea tried to
identify his call. But she couldn't place it. After years
of city living, it was hard to remember the little she
had learned in her childhood about birds. 'I hope
Doris puts up a bird feeder at least,' she told herself
idly. What a waste it would be, in surroundings like
these, not to enjoy nature's bounty.

The scent of the earth and the new green grass
tugged at her. Chelsea's fingers itched to dig into the
warm soil, to pack it around fragile little plants and
nurture them. 'You're just a country girl at heart,' she
scolded herself lightly.

Then playful shrieks from the house next door drew
her attention. Across the ravine, the little girl with the
pigtails was playing with her puppy. They rolled over
and over on the grass, then the child flung a stick and
the dog, ears flying, romped after it.

I want that, Chelsea told herself suddenly. I want all
that she represents—a husband, a home, a child . . .

It wasn't that she didn't like her job; she would
never give it up. But it wasn't enough. Building
houses for other people could never take the place of
building a life for herself.

Sunlight poured down across the hillside in
streaks and caught the child and the dog. They
seemed to freeze into position in the pool of light for
a long moment, then the dog barked and tore off
across the lawn to greet a car as it pulled into the
drive. The little girl followed, and when the car
stopped, she flung herself into the arms of the man
who stepped out.

'Daddy's home,' Chelsea murmured, and tears rose in her eyes.

And you, she scolded herself, are a sentimental fool, to let yourself be carried away by such nonsense. She rose briskly and brushed loose debris off her skirt. It was long past time to go to the hospital, and sitting here any longer could only lead her into dangerous thoughts.

Burke was in the lounge, his tie loose, his jacket tossed aside. His feet were propped up on a chair, and his eyes were closed. He looked every year of his age, today, Chelsea thought, and her heart ached for him. Helen was the dearest thing in his life, and he had no one to help him bear the pain.

He roused suddenly and smiled when he saw her. 'She's better, Chelsea.'

'I'm glad. Have you had some sleep?'

He avoided her eyes. 'Some. They've been letting me stay with her most of the time.'

'Well, I think it's time you got some genuine rest. I'll stay here for a few hours. You go home and sleep, and that's an order.'

'No. I'll be all right.' Burke stood up, yawning. 'It's time for me to go back in. She sleeps most of the time, but she likes to have a hand to hold.'

'Shall I come?'

'Will you? She'd love to see you.'

The intensive care unit was quiet, except for the machinery humming beside each patient. Helen's eyes were closed, but when Burke gently picked up her hand, careful not to disturb the intravenous lines, it seemed to Chelsea that Helen's fingers tightened ever so slightly around his.

It brought tears to Chelsea's eyes again. You have to quit this, she told herself impatiently, or you'll turn into a bowl of mush. I need some sleep, soon, or I'm going to be a zombie.

Burke settled himself in the chair next to the high

hospital bed. 'They make allowances for my age and infirmity,' he joked quietly. 'They usually don't put chairs in here because they don't encourage people to stay long.'

Chelsea folded her arms along the top rail of the bed and stared down at Helen. One corner of the woman's mouth seemed to have a tired droop to it. It was the side that had been affected by the stroke, Chelsea knew, and wondered just how bad the damage would turn out to be.

'Mr Marshall?' A white-uniformed nurse was at the door. 'There's a man here asking to see you. Mr Stanton, I believe he said.' She glanced at the clock and reached for the blood-pressure gauge. Chelsea moved out of her way.

'Nick. That's sweet of the boy,' Burke said. 'If you wouldn't mind, Chelsea—I'd rather just stay here. Would you tell him how much I appreciate his visit?'

Chelsea closed her eyes briefly and gathered all the arguments she could make. But the fact was, Burke was at his wife's bedside, and if he didn't want to leave, no one could force him. Besides, who knew what Nick might say? And if he said anything at all to Burke right now . . . Or if he'd brought Vanessa with him . . .

'I'll be right back,' she said.

Burke gave her a grateful smile. 'Take as long as you want.'

It will only take thirty seconds, Chelsea thought, to tell Nick Stanton what I think of him.

Nick was waiting in the corridor. He was alone, Chelsea saw with relief as she let the heavy door shut behind her.

'Burke asked me to thank you for coming,' she said coolly.

His dark blue eyes summed her up. 'So you're back, hovering beside the deathbed.'

'I told you this morning that with any luck, Helen won't die.'

'Now what makes you say that, I wonder? If you're trying to impress me, don't bother. Your charming devotion to a friend isn't quite convincing.'

'Really, Nick.' Chelsea kept her voice even with an effort. 'Just what would you do for entertainment if I wasn't here to vent your anger against?'

His eyes narrowed. 'Are friends allowed to visit?'

'No.'

'I'll send flowers.'

'Don't bother.' Then she tried to soften the statement. 'They're not allowed in the unit. As soon as she's moved to a room she can have them.'

'How did you manage to get in to see her?'

'Believe it or not, Helen thinks of me as a daughter.'

Nick started to laugh. 'How cosy!'

Chelsea saw red. He had a colossal nerve to say things like that to her, with Vanessa waiting for him in the lobby, or in the car, or at home ... She held her temper with an effort. 'Let's not squabble in the hallway, for heaven's sake.'

'Where would you prefer to do it?'

'Nowhere at all.' She put a hand on the doorway. 'Goodbye, Nick.' It was quiet, and it felt very final. She hadn't told him how furious she was with him, Chelsea realised as she went back to Helen's room, but there would always be time for that.

Helen was awake and trying to swallow some clear broth when Chelsea returned to the little room.

'I'm making a mess of it,' she told Chelsea. The words were understandable, but muddled, and Helen closed her eyes tightly in frustration.

Chelsea thought, Don't give up, Helen. She squeezed the woman's hand and was rewarded by a brief half-smile and a renewed effort to eat. Admiration woke in her. With so many problems, Helen was continuing to fight. And she would overcome this, too.

The nurses finally overruled Burke and sent him

home to sleep. Chelsea stayed much later than she had planned, waiting for Helen to settle down for the night, and it was after midnight when she entered her own apartment.

Judy was pacing the floor. Her hair was in rollers and she was wearing the oversized nightshirt that was her favourite. 'Where have you been?' she demanded. 'I've nearly worn a hole in this carpet, waiting for you.'

Chelsea tossed her handbag on to the hall table. 'At the hospital.'

'Nick said he'd tried to reach you there.'

Chelsea shrugged. 'Perhaps I just didn't hear the page.'

'He wants you to call him, by the way.'

'Oh, he does? I wonder what the dear boy wants this time?' She flung herself down into a chair.

'Are you going to call him?'

'Perhaps.'

Judy just looked at her for a long time. 'Do you want to talk about it?'

'Not right now.'

'Just remember that I'll be gone this weekend. There's a package for you, by the way.' Judy went off down the hall to her bedroom.

Chelsea picked up the package, addressed in her mother's neat, careful hand. She cut the cord and out tumbled a yellow linen dress, tailored with tiny cap sleeves and a narrow belt. She found a note tucked into a fold.

'Stewart's was having a sale,' she read, 'and I thought this would look good on you. We loved having you at home, Chelsea. Come more often. And tell Nick that we enjoyed his visit too. Love, Mom.'

Chelsea shook out the dress and laid it aside. Darn her mother anyway, she thought. From a hundred miles away she could make Chelsea feel guilty. Tell Nick they'd enjoyed his visit, indeed! If she told Nick anything, it certainly wouldn't be that.

Why had Nick called? Chelsea sat there and stared at the telephone. Then, reluctantly, she picked it up. It was all her mother's fault, she thought glumly. Sara was the one who had raised Chelsea to always answer letters, write thank-you notes—and return telephone calls.

Nick's phone rang several times, and then a sleepy female voice answered.

She hadn't even thought about what she would do if Vanessa answered. It must have been only a couple of seconds, but to Chelsea it seemed forever before she heard herself ask, 'Is John there?'

'John?' Vanessa yawned, and then drawled, 'You've got the wrong number. And check it before you dial it again. Some of us are trying to sleep.'

'I'm sorry,' Chelsea said softly and cradled the phone. So Vanessa was in residence. Chelsea hadn't expected that. After the argument she had overheard at Angelo's, she would have thought Vanessa would be staying at a hotel.

They must have come to some agreement about the abortion, and Chelsea found herself wondering what it was. Had Vanessa yielded—with the great charm she undoubtedly possessed—and agreed to give Nick his child? Or had he reluctantly given in to that same charm and consented to allow the abortion?

'I wish I had Vanessa's choice,' Chelsea murmured, and then realised in shock what she had said. She sat down suddenly, hands pressed to her hot cheeks. If she had Vanessa's choice, it would be no choice at all.

'I would be delighted to have Nick's baby,' she said, and the words seemed to echo in the quiet room. 'How long,' she asked herself miserably, 'how long have I been in love with him?'

CHAPTER TEN

IT was a long, lonely weekend. Judy and Jim left early Saturday morning for their visit to Jim's family, and Chelsea spent most of her time at the hospital. When she wasn't there, she was at home, sometimes listening to melancholy music on the stereo, sometimes mindlessly watching television, sometimes just sitting in the darkened rooms, thinking about Nick.

How had she let herself slip into this dreadful muddle? When had her loathing of some of his personal traits faded? When had respect for his skill as an architect evolved into love for the man?

If he'd only been honest with me, she thought, I wouldn't be in this spot. And then, with brutal truthfulness, she admitted that it wouldn't have mattered even if she'd known he was married. Knowing that he had a wife didn't relieve the awful longing in her heart. She still wanted him, whether or not Vanessa was in the way.

How had a man as intelligent as Nick allowed himself to get mixed up with Vanessa, anyway? She raged about that a little. The woman was heartbreakingly lovely, there was no doubt about that. But surely even someone who was infatuated with her beauty could see that there was no soul under that lovely shell, no warmth, no love.

'Come on, Chelsea,' she scolded herself, 'you're more than a bit prejudiced when it comes to the luscious Vanessa.' Perhaps Nick had truly loved the woman. Perhaps—she faced the most awful truth of all—perhaps he still did.

And with that thought dragging her down, she showered and dressed and went back to the hospital, to the only thing that could take her thoughts off Nick.

On Sunday morning they moved Helen to a side ward. The relief in the air was almost visible, and Burke and Chelsea did a quick dance step down the hall when they got the news. The nurses watched them indulgently.

'The therapist will come in tomorrow to start working with you, Mrs Marshall,' one of the nurses told Helen. 'We'll soon have you back on your feet.'

'Telling me that is something like the old joke, you know,' Helen answered weakly. 'The patient asks his doctor if he can dance after his injury heals, and the doctor says of course he can. And the patient says, "That's good, Doc, because I never could before!"' Her speech was improving, and her sense of humour with it. 'I haven't been so great at dancing lately, so I'll settle for ordinary walking.'

But the move wore her out, and she slept most of the day. Mid-afternoon she woke, watched Chelsea quietly for a while, and said, 'What's wrong, dear?'

Chelsea jumped. She had been lost in thought, expecting that Helen would sleep longer. She looked down at the newspaper that lay open on her knee. She'd started out to work the crossword puzzle, but there in the margin was a pencilled sketch of Nick's face. She folded it carefully inside the paper, and said quietly, 'I was just thinking about going back to Norah Springs.'

'A vacation? That would be nice, Chelsea. You need one.'

Chelsea shook her head. 'Not a vacation, Helen. To stay.'

There was utter silence in the room for a moment. Then Burke wheeled around from the window, where he'd been standing, and said, 'You're going to leave Shelby Harris?'

'I'm thinking about it.'

'Why, Chelsea?'

'And I want to try my own wings, Burke. Since I

didn't get the partnership, I think I'll go back to Norah Springs and set up my own practice.' She raised her chin a defiant half-inch.

'It's going to look as though you're a sore loser, Chelsea. You can't fool anyone with that story.'

Had he looked into her heart, Chelsea wondered uneasily.

'Everybody knows you've been deadly jealous of Nick since that partnership came open. Leaving now won't look good on your records, Chelsea.'

'Perhaps it won't,' she said quietly. 'But I really don't care what it looks like, Burke.'

Burke shook his head. 'You'll have to finish your commitments, Chelsea. The houses you still have on the drawing board, the civic centre up in Norah Springs . . .'

'I'll be right on top of that one,' Chelsea said sweetly.

Burke ignored the interruption. 'To say nothing of the Jonas Building.'

'If we win the contest.' Chelsea dismissed the Jonas Building with a wave of her hand.

'From what I've seen, I'd bet on you and Nick.'

She thought about her bet with Nick on the Sullivan house, and allowed herself a brief smile. 'It isn't wise to bet on rumour, Burke. Sometimes the advance sketches bear no resemblance to the finished product.'

'I have my sources,' Burke said stiffly.

'I know. But the deadline for submitting plans isn't till Tuesday. Something wonderful may come in at the last minute.'

'At any rate, whether you win the contest or not, you and Nick are a darned good team, Chelsea. Why do you want to break that up?'

She almost told him. But Burke, sympathetic soul that he was, tried so hard to make things better that he sometimes wasn't wise about his methods. Chelsea knew that if she told Burke why she was leaving, he would try to fix it all up. He'd probably call Nick in and talk to him, and try to straighten the whole mess out.

Chelsea shuddered. That would be the last unbearable straw. So long as Nick didn't know how hopelessly she had fallen in love with him, Chelsea could hold up her head. But if he ever found out——

She sidetracked that train of thought and tried a different approach with Burke. 'No matter when I leave, I'll have a dozen projects in the works,' she pointed out. 'There will never be a time when all my work is done.'

'That's true, but . . .'

'Are you suggesting, perhaps, that Nick isn't capable of taking over a few houses?' Her tone was sweetness itself.

As she had expected, Burke was instantly defensive. 'Of course not. He's the best there is. But——'

'Then I'll leave my work in good hands, won't I?'

A nurse tapped on the door and brought in an amber glass vase filled with yellow and white daisies. 'Mrs Marshall? One of your admirers discovered that you can have flowers now. My goodness, that young man is right on the ball.' She waved the flowers under Helen's nose, arranged them on the bedside table, and handed Chelsea the card with a flourish.

Chelsea tore the little envelope open. 'They're from Nick,' she announced.

'That's sweet of him,' Helen murmured and stretched out her good hand to caress a smooth petal. 'I wonder how he knew that daisies are my favourite.'

'He probably reads minds, along with all of his other superhuman traits,' Chelsea said.

Burke gave her a warning frown.

'If you're determined to move, Chelsea,' Helen said, 'at least we can relieve you of one project. I've decided I don't want to build the new house after all.'

'Helen, are you sure?' Burke asked. 'You haven't even seen the plans.'

She nodded. 'Yes, dear, I'm certain. I've loved Hillhaven for so many years that no other house would feel like home. How can I leave it now? We'll be able to manage, you'll see.'

It was what Chelsea had half-expected. 'Of course we can arrange it, Helen. That little den at the back of the house would work for your bedroom.'

'You don't mind, Chelsea?' Burke asked. 'I'm sorry about putting you to all the work.'

'It's no problem, really. It only took me a few hours, and it was good practice.'

'I'll pay you for the plans, of course.'

Chelsea came as close as she ever had to losing her temper with him. 'I don't want to hear another word about being paid, Burke,' she said sternly. 'I did it because I love you, and that's all the pay I need.'

Burke seemed chastened. 'Very well, Chelsea. If you insist.'

'That's the way it has to be. I think I'll go home now,' she said. 'I have to go to work tomorrow, you know, and I'm worn out.'

'Stop in anytime,' Helen said. 'But don't feel that you have to come, Chelsea. It sounds as if they'll be keeping me busy.'

Chelsea forced a smile. 'Just work hard at that therapy, and you'll be back at Hillhaven even before all your friends have a chance to visit you here.'

'Going home is a good goal,' Helen admitted. 'You aren't hurt about the house?'

'Heavens, no. I suspected that you might change your mind.' She dropped a quick kiss on Helen's cheek and waved goodbye to Burke.

Outside the door, she nearly fell over Nick, who was leaning against the corridor wall. 'So it was a house, and you did it for love,' he said softly. 'Is there anything you wouldn't do for Burke, my dear? For love, of course.'

'Don't you have anything better to do than eavesdrop outside hospital rooms, Nick?' she asked crossly. Why aren't you at home entertaining Vanessa, she wondered, and her heart ached.

'But I find out so many interesting things this way,' he pointed out, and dropped into step beside her as she started down the hall. 'And you even announced your devotion in front of Helen. Don't you feel a bit embarrassed about that?'

'Not in the least.' She looked at him defiantly. 'Why should I?'

'The scandal, of course. Just in case you change your mind about that little discussion we had, I'm still available,' he added. 'See you tomorrow, Chelsea.' He turned back towards Helen's room, leaving her standing, speechless, in the middle of the hall.

The apartment was dark; Judy was not yet home from her weekend trip. Chelsea hated the loneliness. How much her point of view had changed over the last few weeks, since that day when she had half-decided to look for an apartment of her own. Now she longed to have people around, to be kept too busy to think.

She put a frozen pizza in the oven and decided to spend the evening catching up on her professional journals. At least if she was absorbed in her reading, she couldn't be thinking about Nick.

She was still sitting at the dinette two hours later, but she had to admit the results had been mixed. She had turned a lot of pages, but she was glad she didn't have to take a test over the information she had absorbed.

Judy burst in, her dark eyes glowing, and seized Chelsea in a bearhug. 'Look!' she exclaimed, holding out her left hand. 'This is why Jim took me to visit his family!'

Jim had followed, a little more slowly, with Judy's luggage. 'I just wanted to have all of her attention when I proposed,' he told Chelsea modestly.

Chelsea dutifully admired the diamond ring. 'It's beautiful. When's the wedding?'

'Late summer.' Judy was bubbling over with happiness. 'Oh, Chelsea, I'm so happy!'

'I can see that,' Chelsea said gently.

Jim glanced at his watch. 'I'd better get home. See you at the office tomorrow, Chelsea.'

She retreated to her bedroom to let them have some privacy, and stood there in the dark staring out over the asphalt parking lot. One more thread that had held her to St Louis had been broken. She hadn't been looking forward to telling Judy that she was moving out of the city. Judy could not afford the big apartment without a roommate to split the expenses. But once Judy was married, Chelsea would have nothing to feel guilty about when she left.

When she returned to the living room, Judy had thrown herself down on the couch and was holding the new diamond up under the lamp, watching it fracture the light as she turned it back and forth.

'You look very happy,' Chelsea observed.

'Oh, darling, you have no idea! I've always wanted to marry Jim, but I thought I was just a pastime for him. When he proposed, he was so unsure of himself he was just like a little boy, and ...' She paused. 'What's wrong, Chelsea?'

'Nothing. What could be wrong?'

Judy sat up straight. 'Is it Helen?'

'She's much better.'

'Then what ... Oh. The apartment.' Judy bit her lip. 'I'm sorry. I just was so excited by my news that I didn't stop to think what it meant to you.'

'It isn't that, Judy. Really. I was trying to find a way to tell you that I'm leaving the city soon. Very soon, actually.'

'You're leaving St Louis? And the firm?'

'Yes. I'm going back to Norah Springs.'

'Back home? But why, Chelsea?'

Chelsea closed her eyes briefly. She could tell Judy the same story she'd been telling everyone else—but after the tears and laughter they had shared in the five years of their friendship, Judy deserved better than that. 'Because Nick Stanton is married.'

Judy started to laugh. 'And so is the governor of Missouri, but I don't see that influencing . . .' Her voice trailed off. 'You're actually serious, Chelsea!'

Tears burned in Chelsea's eyes. She tried to blink them away, and nodded. 'You were right, when you told me not to play games with him, that he'd hurt me. Well, I hurt myself, Judy.' She wiped the tears out of her eyes. 'Actually, it was pretty funny.'

'It really looks funny,' Judy said. Her voice was crisp.

'I took him to the Top of the Tower and ate lobster to show him that he couldn't afford me. That was a big joke. Next to Vanessa, I'm about as expensive as popcorn at the movies.'

'Vanessa? I didn't know anyone was actually named that.'

'She may not have been born with it, but it certainly fits. She's no amateur when it comes to spending money, that's certain.'

'Is she pretty?'

Chelsea pulled another tissue out of the box. 'Have you looked at the cover of VOGUE lately? That's the type. In fact, that's what she does for a living.'

'A model?' Judy whistled softly. 'She wasn't at that cocktail party. Nobody even said anything about her.'

'She is apparently a deep, dark secret. Nick's secretary didn't look surprised when Vanessa turned up in her office, so she must have known. But that woman doesn't confide in anyone. She even considers the time of day a secret.' She wiped her eyes again.

'None of the others knew, or it would have been all over the office.'

'How does one keep a Vanessa hidden? And why?'

'Apparently Nick didn't think it was anyone's business. Vanessa doesn't live here, anyway.'

Judy kicked off her shoes and curled up with her feet under her on the couch. 'If they're separated, Chelsea,' she began thoughtfully, 'there is such a thing as divorce, you know.'

'I know.' Chelsea's voice was miserable. 'I've thought about it. But Nick doesn't want to marry me, he just wants to have an affair.' She swallowed hard and pressed on. 'Even if he would divorce Vanessa for me . . .' She shook her head. 'I wouldn't want that. If he would leave her for me, then what happens to me next time he finds an attractive woman?'

'That's true. It's a risk.' Judy thought it over, and asked, 'Why doesn't she live here?'

'Her work is in New York, I suppose. One of the larger cities, at least. She certainly can't make much money modelling in St Louis.'

'Then why didn't he move there, instead of joining Shelby Harris? From what Jim says, Nick's good enough that he could work anywhere.'

'How should I know? I suppose he'd rather be one of the shining lights of architecture out here than to be lost in the crowd on the East Coast.'

Judy shrugged. 'It doesn't say too much for the marriage, does it? And if she isn't any more important to him than that . . .'

'She's recently become a lot more important, Judy.' Chelsea blotted tears off her cheeks, then pressed the tissue into a wad and threw it as hard as she could at the wastebasket. 'Vanessa is pregnant. And Nick isn't questioning whether the baby is his.'

'Oh, for heaven's sake, Chelsea. How can you be so calm about it?'

'This is calm?' Chelsea retorted. 'I'd like to bang my

head against that wall, but the landlord would make me pay for the damage.'

'Sorry, Chels.' Judy fought a yawn and lost. 'What a mess.'

'At any rate, that's why I'm going home. I don't dare stay here. I know what a rotten liar he is, and I still want him so badly that I . . . I can't trust myself.' Chelsea methodically began to shred the tissue box. 'I'm going to sit here a while, Judy. Go to bed if you want. You don't have to keep a watch on me; I'm not going to slash my wrists, or do anything crazy.'

'Good. Because no man is worth it.'

It brought a faint smile. 'Not even Jim?'

'No way,' Judy said firmly. 'No man is worth a slashed wrist, or even a banged head. You'll be all right.'

Chelsea's smile wavered. 'I have to be, don't I? I don't have any other choices left.'

Marie's good-morning smile was tinged with malice. Eileen's hello held a smug giggle. And the silence that fell in the employee lounge when Chelsea went in to get her first cup of coffee was too complete to be a coincidence. They knew about Vanessa, and they had drawn their own conclusions about Chelsea, too.

Oh, stop it, she told herself angrily, once she was barricaded in her own office. All those people may have their suspicions, but there is no evidence. On the other hand, if you go around here like a misunderstood Victorian heroine, everybody will know before lunch.

So she put on a cheery smile when she had to face any of them and spent the morning working on the Sullivan house. She'd met the main challenge of combining the best parts of her efficient and practical interior with Nick's dream-castle exterior before the Sullivans had even seen the rough drawings. Mostly it had been a matter of adjusting dimensions in one plan or the other. But now that it was time to finish the plans, there were an unbelievable number of details to fit in.

She was still struggling when Marie came in. 'I'm going to lunch, Miss Ryan. Do you want me to bring you something from the deli?'

She should go out, Chelsea knew. She should make an appearance to convince them that everything was normal. But why bother? Who cared what the office gossips thought? She wouldn't be around much longer to worry about it. Chelsea suddenly felt very tired. 'Please, Marie. Roast beef on rye with horseradish.'

She picked up the electric eraser again and took out the line she had just drawn in. Her idea of an adequate laundry room didn't want to fit anywhere in Nick's drawings. She picked up his floor plans again to see what he'd done with it.

She was working a lengthy maths problem on her calculator when there was a knock on her door. 'Come in,' she called absently, and didn't raise her eyes from the little machine. If I move that wall, she concluded, I can fit the laundry room in here . . .

'One roast beef on rye, with horseradish on the side, coming up.'

'Nick!' She sat absolutely still for a couple of seconds, trying to bank down the wave of joy that had instantly—embarrassingly—sparkled through her. By the time she raised her eyes to his, she was in control again. 'I didn't know you had become a messenger boy for Marie.'

He shrugged. 'I was standing in line at the deli when Marie said you were working through lunch again. I thought we could talk.' He set a brown bag down on her desk. 'I also brought you a salad, so you wouldn't miss out on your green vegetables today, and a carton of milk, because with all that other stuff you're asking for an ulcer.'

What does he want to talk about, she wondered warily.

'On rye, too, as if the sauce wasn't spicy enough,' he scolded.

'They make the best horseradish in the whole city. It's really very mild. Want to try some?'

'I'm having ham and cheese on white, Chelsea.'

'No spirit of adventure,' she sighed.

He raised an eyebrow a fraction, and his big blue eyes held a sudden gleam of humour. Chelsea thought her heart would break with longing, just looking at him.

'Is that a challenge?' he asked.

'Do you ever turn one down?'

'Rarely. Hand over the horseradish.'

She did. 'Is that why you keep asking me to have an affair with you? Because I'm a challenge?' She felt a little breathless.

He slanted a brief look at her and then smeared horseradish gingerly along the edge of his sandwich. 'You certainly are one,' he agreed.

'Hasn't anyone ever held out this long before?'

'Never. Hey, this stuff isn't half bad.'

'I told you.'

'Stop acting superior and drink your milk.'

'I want you to take a look at the Sullivan plans this afternoon. I think I have the problems solved, and we end up with the best of both designs.'

'Ha. That house was perfect just the way I drew it.'

'Without a laundry room? Don't clothes get dirty in your dream world, Nick?'

He looked chastened. 'So I overlooked something. Let's hit the Jonas Building plans this afternoon. They're due at the end of the week.'

Chelsea sighed. 'Must we?'

'What's the problem? Your condos are almost done.'

'Do you really think we're going to win this? We've put two weeks' work into it.'

'Nothing ventured, nothing gained, you know. Besides, how can we lose? Stanton and Ryan—it's an unbeatable combination.'

Chelsea bit her lip. His light-hearted comment seemed to catch at her throat. 'Why not Ryan and Stanton?' she asked, trying to deny the emotion that he'd roused merely by coupling their names. How silly can you be, Chelsea! she scolded herself.

He looked offended. 'That doesn't sound very liberated of you, Chelsea, wanting top billing. After all, I'm the senior partner.'

'You win.' You always win, Nick, she thought miserably. I can't keep fighting you much longer. 'Where do I start?'

The office was quiet, and not even Marie interrupted. Chelsea was making tracings of the condo floors, cleaning up her rough sketches so that Jim could do the final copies. She was beginning to regret the idealism that had made her design each of the condo units separately. If she had only fallen in with the usual procedure, she could have got by with drawing one floor and letting Jim duplicate it.

She'd almost forgotten Nick was even in the office until mid-afternoon, when he stretched, stood up, and said, 'Do you have any tapes lying around for that sound system?'

'In the bottom drawer of my desk.' She didn't even look up.

Cassette tapes rattled, and then Nick said, 'Vivaldi and Brahms with a sprinkling of hard rock and Dixieland jazz. You're a woman who can't make up her mind, aren't you?'

'No. I just enjoy variety.'

'Isn't that what I said?' The tape player clicked on and started to play a jazz number. Nick adjusted the volume and went back to his work.

For the rest of the afternoon they took turns choosing music, and the soothing strains seemed to speed the work along. The regular office noises subsided as Marie and the rest of the staff went home, and still Nick and Chelsea stayed, absorbed in the drawings. Chelsea's tracings were nearly completed when Nick said, 'Shall we break for dinner? I'll take you to Angelo's.'

'No.' Then, thinking that it hadn't been necessary to be quite so abrupt, Chelsea added, 'I'm almost finished.'

'Whatever you want.' He didn't seem upset, but Chelsea had to make a real effort to get her mind back on her work. She knew it would be foolish to go anywhere with him. Whether he behaved himself or not, she would only be hurt deeper by the memories of dinners when she hadn't yet known about Vanessa, when her love for him had been quietly growing. But another part of her would have gladly suffered any amount of pain to have that last evening with him.

It was growing late when Nick put in yet another Dixieland cassette, dropped the classical one they'd been listening to back in the drawer, and crossed the room to stand behind Chelsea. 'What I don't understand is this—if you like variety so well, why are you still saying no to me?' His hands rested lightly on her shoulders.

'Perhaps I just don't like people who pull rank on me,' she said. She was tired. She wanted only to go home.

'Come on. You never believed those threats, did you?'

'They sounded very realistic.' Chelsea rubbed a hand across the tight muscles at the nape of her neck.

'I would never have given those drawings to Carl. Besides, you could publish that cartoon in the local newspaper and he'd grit his teeth and smile, because he knows very well he can't afford to lose you.'

'I wouldn't like to test that idea.' Chelsea was staring at the paper on her drawing board. Her fingers were clenched on her pencil.

Nick unfolded her fingers and laid the pencil aside.

'Let's test this one, then, shall we?' He tipped her face up, his hand under her chin.

'You don't do things like this in the office,' she protested faintly.

'You drive all sense from my mind, Chelsea,' he said, very softly. His mouth was warm and firm and gentle, and the kiss teased at her senses. 'You taste like horseradish,' he murmured, against her lips, and kissed her again.

This is madness, she thought, and felt as if she were two people—the Chelsea who wanted to hold him close and kiss him with all the longing and love she possessed, but also the Chelsea who stood back and said, Remember Vanessa. Remember the baby . . .

She pulled away, feeling as if she was leaving her heart behind in his arms.

'Chelsea?' he questioned.

'Get away from me,' she ordered. Her voice was taut. 'Don't ever put a finger on me again, Nick Stanton. Do you hear me?'

'Loud and clear,' he agreed. He stalked back across the room to his drawings.

Her hands were shaking. She picked up her pencil, and then laid it aside. It's over, Chelsea, she thought. It's all over.

She sat there for a long time, making meaningless marks on a piece of scrap paper. She didn't want to leave, that was the problem, she realised. Even with the heavy atmosphere in the room just now, there was joy for her just in knowing that he was there, in seeing the sure movements of his pencil from across the room, in watching the set of his shoulders and the way he occasionally ran a hand back over the rumpled dark hair.

She wasn't even angry any more, just very sad. How dreadful it must be for him, she thought. Married to someone who didn't even want to live with him—and obviously caring very much about her. If he didn't love Vanessa, he would have left her; sentiment wasn't a part of Nick's character. In his own way, Chelsea realised, he was faithful to his wife. It didn't make the pain any easier to bear.

Finally she said, 'These are ready for Jim to start on in the morning, Nick. I'm going home.'

'Wait just a minute. Most of mine are finished, too. I just have to put the titles on this one.'

She watched as he labelled the main scale drawing in swift, sure strokes. The Jonas Building, Shelby Harris and Associates of St Louis, Missouri, she read over his shoulder. Below that, in smaller letters, he wrote Nicholas Stanton, Architect. Then for the first time his pen hesitated. 'Chelsea or C.J.?' he asked. 'You've signed your plans both ways.'

'Chelsea.' And she watched as he added her name directly under his. Not as a mere assistant, she saw through misty eyes, but as a partner.

For the first time, she found herself hoping, almost praying, that their design would win. For if it did, then their names would be linked together in the Jonas Building for all time. Future students of architecture would know that the Jonas renovation had been done by Stanton and Ryan.

It would be some kind of comfort, she thought, some sort of immortality for her love, to have their names remembered together, even if she never again saw this man she loved.

CHAPTER ELEVEN

'SHALL we have dinner at the club tonight, dear?' Sara Ryan brought the coffeepot over and refilled Chelsea's cup.

Dinner. I wish I'd had dinner with him that one last time, Chelsea thought. There wouldn't have been anything wrong with that. If only she had some real memories, not just these haunting dreams to keep hidden away forever in the back of her mind.

'Chelsea?' Her mother's tone was sharp.

'Dinner? Whatever you and Dad plan will be fine.'

Sara stared at her daughter, bit her lip, and sighed. Then she pulled a chair out across the table from Chelsea and sat down. 'Chelsea Jean Ryan,' she said, and her tone would have brought Marco Polo back from China. 'You have been home for almost two weeks now, and it's as if we're living with a ghost. What is the matter with you?'

'It's . . . overwork, I suppose, Mom.'

Sara gave a genteel little snort. 'I believed that for the first two days. But you've now had two weeks of relaxation and square meals. Instead of gaining weight and getting a tan, you're even thinner and paler than when you came. You obviously haven't slept in three days, Chelsea.'

'Do I look that good?' Chelsea wisecracked.

Sara frowned. 'It seems to me that you're suffering from depression.'

'Well, I'm not,' Chelsea said shortly. 'I'm just . . .' She didn't know how to go on.

'Waiting? For what?' Sara asked. 'Just when are you planning to start doing something?'

'I thought you wanted me to come home, Mother.'

'I do, Chelsea. I love having you here. But you are so obviously unhappy, dear. You're used to being busy. If you'd just make some plans for your future——'

'I have. I talked to Dad about renting that office in his building.'

'I know. But that was the night you came home, and you haven't been down there to look at it. You haven't the foggiest notion what you'll need to set up your practice.'

'What does it take to be an architect, Mom?' Chelsea asked, a bit cynically. 'A drawing board, a few sheets of paper, a couple of pencils and a client here and there.'

Sara ignored her. 'And you spend most of the day in your room. You haven't even enjoyed the pool.'

Chelsea flared, 'I don't want to lie beside the pool and think——' She stopped abruptly.

Sara let the silence lengthen. 'Think about what, Chelsea?' she asked gently. 'Why did you come home, honey? It was so sudden. Something is terribly wrong . . .'

You are so correct, Mom, Chelsea thought. What's wrong is that he's haunting me. Do you think I haven't tried to get him out of my mind? I can't even pick up a pencil, because when I do, it automatically draws his face. I can't lie out there beside the pool without remembering the first time he kissed me. I can't bear to think of a life without him, and so I don't even want to think at all. Can you understand that, Mother?

But she said nothing. She didn't want to explain it all, and so she chose to share none of it.

'I'll go look at the office, Mom.' Her voice was quiet and almost lifeless.

Sara sat there silently for a while, drinking her coffee. Finally she gave up, and Chelsea quietly went out to the gallery, to fling herself in a hammock and think some more.

Sara was right. Chelsea didn't blame her mother for being concerned. She knew quite well that she had been nothing more than a worry to both Josh and Sara for the last two weeks, with her moping about and her inattention to detail and her sleeplessness. She couldn't even carry on a conversation.

Perhaps she shouldn't have come home at all, she thought. Nick haunted this place, too, and her parents' concern was only leading Chelsea to a morbid suspicion that there might be something wrong with her mind.

At the very least, she should not have come home in the middle of the night like that. Sara suspected that something dreadful had happened, she knew, and she didn't know how to tell her mother that she had been running only from herself.

She and Nick had left the office together, after the Jonas Building drawings had been completed, and walked out to the parking ramp. That was all. He had said a curt goodnight as he left her unlocking the Mercedes, and he'd gone on to his car. Chelsea had held herself together till she was away from the ramp, but then the tears started to flow, the tears of hopelessness and sadness and heartbreak. She had gone back to the apartment, but it was empty, so she packed a few clothes, left a note for Judy, and started home to Norah Springs.

She would never forget the shock on her father's face when he had opened the door that night. It was the only thing that had brought laughter. She had asked him about the office, and then gone straight to bed, certain that the long drive, coming after the longer day, would bring welcome oblivion. But she had not slept.

Reluctantly, the next morning, she had called the office, hoping that Nick would not be there. She had her message all planned and rehearsed, but hearing his voice had thrown her into disarray. 'What is it,

Chelsea?' he had asked, and she had stammered out her answer.

'I'm not feeling well, Nick. I need a couple of weeks to rest, or I'm going to break down entirely.'

He had been silent for a long time, and Chelsea had finally summoned up all her courage and added, 'That wasn't entirely true, Nick. The truth is that I won't be coming back at all. I'll mail you my resignation.'

'Why, Chelsea?'

'Nick, I don't think my reasons are any of your concern.'

'Then you had damn well better think about it again,' he had said coldly. He had still been talking when she hung up on him. She had mailed the letter, which said only that she wasn't coming back and that she hoped the partners would understand why she couldn't give notice. She had dropped it in the mailbox on the corner, and washed her hands of St Louis, and Shelby Harris and Associates, and Nicholas Stanton, with relief.

And then she had gone home and dreamed of him, and awakened drenched with tears.

Perhaps her mother was right, she thought. If she forced herself to do something—anything at all—perhaps tomorrow there would be something she wanted to do. It was worth a try. There must be some activity that would require so much concentration that there would be no room left in her thoughts for Nick. Inaction certainly hadn't helped; perhaps action would.

The telephone rang, and her heart began to pound. When Sara came to the door, Chelsea was already shaking her head.

'It's Judy,' Sara said. She looked worried.

Chelsea pushed herself up out of the hammock. Stupid, she thought. Utterly silly to be frightened every time the phone rang. It could ring hundreds of times, and it would not be Nick.

'Hi, Judy.'

'Chelsea? Sara says you're wasting away to bare bones.'

Chelsea glanced over her shoulder to make sure her mother wasn't within hearing. 'You didn't tell her, did you?'

'About Nick? No, but I'm regretting that I promised not to tell her,' Judy countered. 'Silence certainly is doing you no good.'

'It's my business, Judy.'

'Well, that's absolutely correct. Just as long as you haven't wasted into a ghost by the time I get married. We moved the date up, by the way. Will you be a bridesmaid?'

'Sure.' Chelsea wished that she could work up some enthusiasm. 'Judy—is there any news?' She hated herself for even asking.

'About Nick, you mean? I shouldn't do this, but Jim said to tell you that he's been a real bear lately.'

'Did the Jonas drawings make the deadline?'

'Yes. And Jim packed up all of your personal things and brought them to the apartment. All except your mug.'

'My crystal one? What happened to it?'

'He said Nick lost an account the other day and he picked up your mug and threw it at the wall.'

'At least he didn't throw it at me,' Chelsea muttered.

'From what Jim saw, Nick would have liked to. There were too many pieces to pick up.'

'I ought to send him a bill. That was a birthday present, dammit. He had no right to break my crystal mug!'

'Go get him, tiger,' Judy applauded. 'At least there's some life in your voice now. When are you coming back?'

'Next week maybe, just long enough to pick up my things. I'll see you then.'

'All right. Jim and I will take you out for pizza.'

'Thanks, Judy.' Her voice was softer, and she was actually smiling when she cradled the phone.

Activity. That was the key. She felt as if the last two weeks had been a bad dream, and that she had just awakened. She refused to let Nick Stanton turn her into a recluse. 'I'm going to walk down to the office,' she called to her mother, and left the house without waiting for an answer.

The streets were quiet, the breeze whispering along the shaded lanes and tugging at the locks of Chelsea's hair, left to flow loose down her back. It was mid-June now, and summer had matured since she had come home. The leaves were huge and brilliant green on the maples. The sun lay hot on the asphalt streets, and children's laughter echoed across the lawns.

Chelsea turned towards the centre of town. She noticed a sign in an upstairs window that offered an apartment for rent. She supposed she would soon have to look for a place to live. Much as she loved her parents, it wasn't healthy to continue to stay with them. 'You're going to have to grow up someday, Chelsea,' she muttered, and turned down a side street to the quiet brick building that held her father's law practice.

His secretary was grey-haired, correct, utterly discreet, the perfect legal assistant. She looked Chelsea over with a raised eyebrow, and seemed to focus on her clothes. 'May I help you, Miss Ryan?' she asked.

The woman had always been able to make her feel inadequate, Chelsea thought. A spark of rebelliousness rose in her. What business of hers was it what Chelsea chose to wear? The faded old jeans were just right for climbing about in an empty building.

'I stopped to get the key for the office next door. And do you happen to have a tape measure? I forgot mine.'

The secretary fished the keys out of her desk. 'Mr

Ryan said some time ago that you'd be coming in,' she observed.

'And now I'm here,' Chelsea said sweetly. She held out her hand for the keyring.

'I'm afraid I haven't anything to measure with. This is a legal office, you see—not a construction company.'

Chelsea thanked her gravely and went back out to the sidewalk. As she let herself into the empty office, she told herself grimly, 'If I'm going to work next door to that woman, we are going to collide.'

The idea actually had some appeal. It was the first time in a week that she had felt any particular interest in anything.

The office smelled musty. It had been shut up for some time. Chelsea paced off the length of the reception room and wished that she had asked for paper and pencil. The secretary would probably have told her that she didn't have any to spare, Chelsea thought spitefully.

There were two small offices at the back, a tiny bathroom, and a hidden exit. 'Trust Dad,' she said. 'He would never have an office anywhere that didn't allow him to avoid the waiting clients on his way to the handball court!'

She would have liked to design this office complex. But it had been completed while she was still in college. Maybe someday I'll have my own, she thought. My own offices, with a sign above the door that reads Ryan and Stan . . .

She pulled herself up short, the ache in her throat almost choking her, and stood there gritting her teeth against the pain. Nick's name had come so automatically to her tongue that it frightened her. 'Chelsea Ryan and Associates,' she said firmly. Her voice seemed to echo in the empty room.

Well, for right now it would be Chelsea Ryan without associates. She would even have to be her own draughtsman at first, until the business started to build. That part of it she wouldn't like at all.

She paced off the rooms. She'd have to come back with a tape and get the exact dimensions before she could even look at furniture. A desk and chair would probably be all she needed, for right now. Her drawing board was still in St Louis, at the apartment. Some filing cabinets, perhaps. It would take little enough to get started.

'Chelsea?' her father called from the front door. 'Are you in here?'

'Sure, Dad.' She came out of the back office, brushing dust off her hands. 'Don't you believe in cleaning ladies?'

'Not for empty buildings.' The relief on his face when he saw her smile touched Chelsea's heart. 'Have lunch with me? I'll buy you a tenderloin and fries at the club.'

Chelsea smiled. It was the bribe he had always offered in her childhood. 'French fries are in violation of my diet, Dad. Besides, they won't let me in. I'm wearing jeans.'

'We can go to the grill. And I'll let you have a salad instead of the fries.'

If he says anything about eating my green vegetables, Chelsea thought, I'll start to cry. You are such a sentimental fool, she told herself sternly. You can't give up lettuce forever just because Nick once bought you a salad.

For the first time, she made a real effort to bury him in the back of her mind. Josh seemed to recognize her struggle, and he exerted himself to be charming. By the time they left the country club, Chelsea's sides ached from laughing, and she felt more like her old self than she had in weeks.

'I'll drive you home,' Josh offered.

'I can walk if you have something important to do.'

He shook his head. 'I'm just playing tennis this afternoon.'

'Oh. The truth is, you have to go home to change clothes anyway.'

'Something like that,' he agreed.

The sun roof was open on his sports car today, and the breeze tugged at Chelsea's hair. It felt good. She thought about taking the Mercedes out this afternoon, putting the top down, and then speeding along the country roads.

Or perhaps while new ambition was still bubbling, she should measure the office and go look at furniture. Tomorrow she might find herself in the dumps again.

No, she decided. She wasn't going to be in the dumps any more. She had wasted too many days now in mourning Nick Stanton. It would take a long time to get over him, she knew, but she didn't have to hide herself away from the world to grieve.

Her mother was on the gallery with Elise Bradley. They were drinking coffee, and between them on the table was a watercolour of a sailboat on a lake. It had been painted by Elise, Chelsea diagnosed the instant she saw it. Sara had never painted anything so awful in her life.

'Hello, dear,' her mother said. 'Nick called right after you left.'

Chelsea swallowed hard. 'Oh?' She nodded a greeting at Elise.

'The number is beside the kitchen phone. I told him you'd call him at the office as soon as you came in.'

'I wonder if it's about the civic centre,' Elise speculated. 'Or perhaps it's something else.' Her tone was sly. 'I must say, Chelsea, everybody expected when you came home that Nick would spend his weekends here at least.'

'Why should he?' Chelsea asked quietly.

Elise tittered. 'It was fairly obvious, my dear. The two of you made such a cute couple. Didn't they, Sara?'

'I'm afraid I didn't pay any attention.' Sara pushed a plate across the table. 'Have another cookie, Elise.'

'Oh, I shouldn't. But . . .'

'Have you talked to your kids lately?' Sara pressed on ruthlessly. 'Will they be home this summer?'

Thank God for mothers to come to the rescue, Chelsea thought, and went down the hall to her room. What could Nick want now, she wondered. He should have received her resignation letter ten days ago, and there had been nothing but silence ever since. She couldn't imagine why he would be calling now. But if it wasn't her resignation, what could it be?

She almost didn't make the phone call, but she knew that Sara would catch up with her later if she didn't. She was shaking as she listened to the clicks as her call traced through the electronic jungle to Nick's office. And her voice trembled as she asked for him.

But his secretary said he wasn't there. 'He didn't tell me where he was going, Miss Ryan. I think perhaps he's out on the construction sites.'

'Thanks. Tell him I called.' Chelsea put the phone down, feeling as if she had broken her last connection with him.

Then she tried to shake herself out of the mood. Time to do something daring, she thought, and put on a brief swimsuit. Someday she was going to have to face that swimming pool. It might as well be today.

The water lay still and cool under the blazing sun. Chelsea dived in and swam laps as fast as she could, trying to tire herself out. Exhaustion came far sooner than she had expected, and she sat breathing hard on the edge of the pool for a few minutes, trying to recover. 'You're out of shape, Chelsea Ryan,' she told herself glumly, and reached for her sunscreen lotion. Wasn't talking to oneself the first classic symptom of mental disorder?

'The shape still looks pretty good to me,' a husky voice said behind her.

Chelsea turned around and lost her balance. She had to grab at the edge of the pool to keep from falling in. She pushed her wet hair back off her forehead and whispered, 'Nick? Oh, my God, now I'm having hallucinations.'

But the man standing at the edge of the pool beside her didn't look like a delusion. Instead he looked tough, as handsome as ever, and very substantial indeed.

'You're not seeing things, Chelsea. I'm really here.'

'Why?' she whispered.

He smiled faintly. 'Because I'm the most junior of the senior partners, I suppose. I've been covering for you for two weeks, Chelsea, but . . .'

'Well, isn't that sweet of you.' Her voice dripped sarcasm. She ignored his outstretched hand and got to her feet by herself. She pulled on her towelling robe and lay down on the chaise, her eyes closed. 'I'm so grateful.'

'If you'd let me finish my sentence, Chelsea?'

She shrugged and kept her eyes closed.

'Nobody else in that office can do your job. Hell, any two of us couldn't keep up with your work.'

'I told you I was overworked and exhausted.'

'I even lost the Sullivans. They decided to buy stock blueprints from some service in California, and build an ordinary split-level.'

'Is that why you broke my crystal mug?' She glanced up and saw the surprise on his face. 'I still have sources, Nick.'

He was silent. Finally Chelsea said, 'I half-expected they'd do that.'

He sighed. 'I suppose I should have seen it coming. It's cheaper—at least it looks that way at the beginning. And old Charlie does keep a close eye on his dollar.'

'It wasn't the money, Nick. It was the house. We drew it for each other, not for the Sullivans.' Then, as she heard what she had said, Chelsea flushed and squirmed a little in her chair. 'I mean, we had our eyes on the competition, not on the what the clients wanted. Of course they didn't like it; it wasn't their kind of house.' She lay back with a sigh and looked up at him. 'I couldn't have held them either, Nick. Don't blame yourself.'

He rubbed a hand across the back of his neck. 'I could shoot myself for interfering. If I'd left you alone, you could have done something fantastic for them.'

'Did you come up here to tell me that?'

'No. I came up to ask you to come back to work. What do you want, Chelsea? What arrangements can we make?'

She closed her eyes and let the silence lengthen. Finally she said, her voice so weary that there was no room for emotion, 'I want to be left alone. I don't want to see you again, Nick.'

'Look, I'm sorry it had to be me. But I could hardly tell Carl Shelby, when he asked me to come, why I didn't think you'd listen to me. So please just pretend I'm someone else and listen to what I have to say.'

Pretend he was someone else? When every sensitive nerve ending knew exactly where he was, and how close to her, even when her eyes were closed? When her hands, with a mind of their own, wanted to reach out to him and pull him down beside her on the lounger?

'So sit down and say it,' she murmured.

'I'm a heel.' He pulled a lounge chair up opposite hers.

'You certainly are.'

'A rotten scum.'

'That, too.'

He ran a hand through his hair. 'A misguided fool.'

'Absolutely.'

'At least we now have something we agree on,' he said, with a half-humorous note in his voice. 'What do you need to make you come back to the firm, Chelsea? A raise? An assistant? Two assistants?'

'No. No. And no.'

He went on ruthlessly. 'A partnership?'

'They are desperate, aren't they?' she asked curiously. She didn't look at him.

'Ive been authorised to give you anything you want, Chelsea.'

Except the one thing I want most, and that one I can't have, she thought. 'No, Nick.'

'I need you to help design the civic centre for Norah Springs.'

'What is this, Nick? A sudden attack of humility? It doesn't sound like you. Take two aspirins—you'll feel better in the morning.'

There was a brief silence. 'There is one more thing you should know. We won the Jonas competition.'

She opened her eyes at that. 'I haven't seen it in the papers.'

'And you won't for a while. It isn't official yet; they just called me this morning.'

'Is that the real reason you came up here?'

'It's part of it,' he admitted. 'I need you, Chelsea. I can't do it without you.'

She shook her head. 'That's not true, Nick. Any competent builder can read those blueprints. You certainly can.'

'Could you carry it through, when you're half of a team?' He paused, and added quietly, 'If you don't come back, I will forfeit the contest.'

'On purpose?' She studied his face. 'No, you won't, Nick. It means too much to you.'

'You still won't come? Why Norah Springs, Chelsea?'

She looked around as if curious herself. 'I'm a country girl at heart. And I'm tired of the pace in the city, and the workload. Is that reason enough?'

'When you put it that way,' he admitted, 'I almost want to join you. Is your decision final?'

'Yes.' Goodbye, my love, she wanted to say.

He sighed and ran a hand through already rumpled hair. 'I imagine Burke will try to persuade you.'

'He's welcome to try. In case you're worried about how you stand with Carl Shelby, you can relax. Burke won't be able to convince me either.' Then she realised abruptly that there had not been even a hint of sarcasm in his voice.

'Helen sent you her love,' Nick added.

She sat up slowly. 'Don't tell me. You finally figured out that Burke and I are not having an affair.'

A half-smile tugged at the corner of his mouth. 'Burke convinced me.'

'How did he do it? I've tried for weeks.'

Nick said reluctantly, 'I finally confronted him about it. He laughed till I thought he was going to have a heart attack.'

'That's hardly flattering,' Chelsea mused. 'But I suppose if it worked, I should be thankful.'

'Even Burke thinks you should give me a second chance.'

'I trust Burke doesn't know all the details. Tell Carl that I really appreciate the offer, Nick.'

'They'd rather have you than your appreciation.'

She shook her head.

Nick sighed. 'I guess that's that. I brought these back.' He dropped an envelope in her lap.

She opened it, and the caricatures slid out on to the table. 'No more blackmail?'

'No. I want you to come back with me, but not that way.'

'That's generous.' She flipped through the pile. 'One is missing, Nick.' She could see it in her mind, the sketch of Mount Rushmore with Nick as one of the great stone faces.

'I didn't think you'd begrudge me that one, Chelsea.'

She swallowed hard. 'Keep it, if you like,' she said.

'But as long as we're talking about personal property—you still have the top of my swimsuit.' She fought against the blush that was rising in her cheeks.

'Sorry. That's a souvenir of a very special woman.'

'Nick, give it back. It . . .'

'Chelsea, let me finish. Please?'

She sighed and leaned back in her chair, her eyes closed. 'Help yourself.'

There was a catch in his voice as he said, 'Thanks for the invitation. I think I'll do that.' An instant later, she felt his weight on the side of her chair, and before she could struggle or even catch her breath, he was kissing her with a gentle fierceness that sent lightning flickering along every nerve.

She couldn't stop herself. If she had had a chance to prepare for the onslaught, she might have exercised iron self-control. But instead, her will power shattered under that sudden, demanding kiss. She found herself responding gladly to the pressure of his mouth, and eagerly accepting his caresses when he impatiently pushed aside the towelling robe.

'I knew I was right, Chelsea,' he whispered, as his mouth brushed her earlobe. 'We are magic together. There's a certain something between us . . .'

And her name was Vanessa. The thought echoed through Chelsea's mind. Then she braced both hands against his chest and pushed as hard as she could.

Nick was stunned. 'What's wrong, darling?'

'Don't call me that,' Chelsea said between clenched teeth. She struggled out of the chair and stood at the edge of the pool, her head up, staring at him with defiance. 'Get out of here, Nick,' she warned, 'or I will scream.' She was breathing hard.

'Why?' he demanded. 'Just answer that for me, Chelsea. How can you turn your back on what we share?'

'Oh, you poor innocent dear,' she mocked. 'And just what would we share, if I came back? An office every day? A bed every night—except when Vanessa comes to town?' Her voice rose sharply till she was almost screaming at him. 'And what am I supposed to do then, Nick? Pretend that I don't know you? Call you Mr Stanton and exchange social chit-chat at the office parties with your wife?'

'Oh, my God,' he said.

'You didn't expect Vanessa to show up, did you?'

'Vanessa's chief charm is her unpredictability,' he agreed. 'Nobody ever expects anything from Vanessa. That way they are seldom disappointed.'

'I don't know what kind of a marriage that is, but I want no part of it.'

He sat down in the lounge chair and linked his hands behind his head. 'Is that why you were so cold those last few days? Vanessa?'

She was stunned. 'Isn't that enough reason?'

'So Burke was right. He thought that you were attracted to me. But I was sure you couldn't forgive me for thinking that you'd slept your way into that job. Funny, that I could be so blind,' he mused.

'Absolutely hilarious,' Chelsea muttered.

'I didn't even realise what was happening to me. It was plain old jealousy, Chelsea. I didn't just want to sleep with you; I wanted all of you—heart and soul as well as body.'

Her whole body was throbbing with the rhythm of his words. 'Go to hell, Nick Stanton!'

'I'll give you back the swimsuit top when you marry me,' he said. His tone was conversational.

'Didn't you hear me, Nick?'

'I heard you. Being married to a redhead just might be hell on earth—but I'm willing to risk it. Because, you see, I love you, Chelsea.'

'I will not marry a man who divorces his wife for me, Nick. I'd be afraid that the next time a pretty face came along——'

'Vanessa is my sister-in-law,' he said quietly.

'He'd divorce me, too. My God, Nick, she's pregnant! What did you say?'

'Vanessa is my brother's wife,' he said, enunciating each word carefully. 'She's Mrs Stanton, all right. Mrs Nate Stanton.'

Chelsea sat down, hard, in her lounge chair.

Nick smiled at her equably. 'There's a Mrs Miles Stanton, too. She's my other brother's wife. Just because you are an only child doesn't mean everybody is, Chelsea.' His tone was fond.

Judy had told her that, she thought. She had said something at that long-ago cocktail party at Hillhaven about Nick being one of three brothers. Chelsea vaguely remembered making a flip comment about the difficulty of dealing with Nick Stanton in triplicate . . .

Nick smiled angelically at her and went on, 'And then of course there's my mother. I must warn you that as Mrs Stanton you'll be one-fourth of a remarkable group. But you'll be the only Chelsea. And you'll always be the only one I want.'

'Why did she . . .' Chelsea swallowed hard and started over. 'Why did she come to you? Vanessa, I mean—about the abortion?'

He raised an eyebrow.

'I heard you talking about it at Angelo's,' Chelsea admitted.

'I see. Do you know, if we could come up with a lightweight material that is truly soundproof we could sell the manufacturing rights and retire wealthy?'

'I don't care, Nick. Tell me about Vanessa.'

'She was trying out the idea on me before she broke it to Nate.'

'It isn't your baby?' Chelsea whispered.

He looked offended. 'You have obviously never met my big brother. The expression is not simply a matter of birth order, you see. He outweighs me by thirty pounds. I am not crazy enough to tangle with Nate, Chelsea. Certainly not over Vanessa.'

She was shivering, despite the heat. She ducked her head and put her hands to her hot cheeks.

Nick glanced at his watch and stood up. 'Well, if we have everything straightened out,' he said calmly, 'I'd better be on my way back to St Louis. Unless you plan to offer me a reason to stay.' His eyes were disturbingly warm.

'Dinner at the country club?' she whispered.

He shook his head firmly. 'Not good enough. You're a tease, Chelsea Ryan.'

She held out a hand, and he pulled her to her feet. 'Will you come back to work?' he asked, suddenly serious.

Chelsea nodded. 'I did want to come home, to be on my own, Nick. But I would never have left if it hadn't been for you. To be near you, but not with you—I couldn't bear that.' Her voice broke as she finished the confession.

He pulled her close, and for the first time Chelsea went into his arms willingly, tugging his head down, clasping her hands at the back of his neck. 'I love you, Nick,' she whispered as her lips met his.

They were both trembling by the time he loosened his hold. 'That will do for a reason to stay,' he said, and laughed shakily. 'As a matter of fact, just try to get rid of me now!'

She let her fingers wander through his disordered dark hair. His hands were warm on the curve of her waist, under the towelling robe. 'Chelsea—if you want to come back to Norah Springs . . .'

She shook her head. 'Wherever you are is good enough for me, Nick.'

'The Jonas Building will take a couple of years. It will give us a chance to build a reputation as a team, and then, if you want, we can move up here.'

'Could we?'

'Of course. We'll be working all over the country anyway. And this must be a great place to raise kids.'

He laughed delightedly as the hot colour swept over her face. 'Chelsea, you're going to have to stop doing that. When my brothers find out how easy it is to make you blush, they'll never let you have a moment of peace.'

'And build a house, Nick? Our house?'

'If you like. It will take at least a couple of years for us to agree on the drawings.'

She let that one pass. 'And we'll start our own firm, too. I can see it now, Ryan and Stanton ...' She darted a playful look up at him.

He frowned. 'Stanton and Ryan,' he countered, and then kissed her. 'Or better yet, Stanton and Stanton. Then nobody will ever know who comes first. Not even us.'

'It will do,' Chelsea murmured, and put her head down on his shoulder.

Coming Next Month in Harlequin Presents!

839 BITTER ENCORE—Helen Bianchin
Nothing can erase the memory of their shared passion. But can an estranged couple reunite when his star status still leaves no room for her in his life—except in his bed?

840 FANTASY—Emma Darcy
On a secluded beach near Sydney, a model, disillusioned by her fiancé, finds love in the arms of a stranger. Or is it all a dream—this man, this fantasy?

841 RENT-A-BRIDE LTD—Emma Goldrick
Fearful of being forced to marry her aunt's stepson, an heiress confides in a fellow passenger on her flight from Denver—never thinking he'd pass himself off as her new husband!

842 WHO'S BEEN SLEEPING IN MY BED?—Charlotte Lamb
The good-looking playwright trying to win her affection at the family villa in France asks too many questions about her father's affairs. She's sure he's using her.

843 STOLEN SUMMER—Anne Mather
She's five years older, a friend of the family's. And he's engaged! How can she take seriously a young man's amorous advances? Then again, how can she not?

844 LIGHTNING STORM—Anne McAllister
A young widow returns to California and re-encounters the man who rejected her years before—a man after a good time with no commitments. Does lightning really strike twice?

845 IMPASSE—Margaret Pargeter
Unable to live as his mistress, a woman left the man she loves. Now he desires her more than ever—enough, at least, to ruin her engagement to another man!

846 FRANGIPANI—Anne Weale
Her sister's offer to find her a millionaire before they dock in Fiji is distressing. She isn't interested. But the captain of the ship finds that hard to believe....

Readers rave about
Harlequin American Romance!

"...the best series of modern romances
I have read...great, exciting, stupendous,
wonderful."
— S.E.,* Coweta, Oklahoma

"...they are absolutely fantastic...going to be
a smash hit and hard to keep on the
bookshelves."
— P.D., Easton, Pennsylvania

"The American line is great. I've enjoyed
every one I've read so far."
— W.M.K., Lansing, Illinois

"...the best stories I have read in a long
time."
— R.H., Northport, New York

*Names available on request.

You're invited to accept 4 books and a surprise gift **Free!**

Acceptance Card

Mail to: Harlequin Reader Service®

In the U.S.
2504 West Southern Ave.
Tempe, AZ 85282

In Canada
P.O. Box 2800, Postal Station A
5170 Yonge Street
Willowdale, Ontario M2N 6J3

YES! Please send me 4 free Harlequin American Romance® novels and my free surprise gift. Then send me 4 brand new novels as they come off the presses. Bill me at the low price of $2.25 each —an 11% saving off the retail price. There are no shipping, handling or other hidden costs. There is no minimum number of books I must purchase. I can always return a shipment and cancel at any time. Even if I never buy another book from Harlequin, the 4 free novels and the surprise gift are mine to keep forever.

154 BPA-BPGE

Name _____ (PLEASE PRINT)

Address _____ Apt. No.

City _____ State/Prov. _____ Zip/Postal Code

This offer is limited to one order per household and not valid to present subscribers. Price is subject to change. ACAR-SUB-1

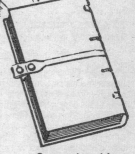